Indie's lost her pet lobster!

"I can't find him," I say as Mom scoops me into a hug.

"What happened?" she says.

"He must've got into my backpack," I say, breaking from her arms and heading back into the water. "Monty!" I spit out some salt water as Mom comes into the ocean, too. "Then I thought I would bring him for a quick dunk to get cool, but he got spooked."

I look over at Officer Gallson, who just stands around looking useless, chewing his gum and putting his hands on his belt like he owns the place.

"It's all his fault!" I shout, pointing right at him. "Your siren scared him."

Mr. Gallson laughs, and I want to run at him and punch him one, but Mrs. Barkley turns me gently toward the water and we scan the whole bay, back and forth from one end of Crawdad Beach to the other. But we don't find him. We search and search until school lets out, and we still don't find him. He's in the sea. He's a golden lobster without a crusher claw. He might as well be a bull's-eye.

OTHER BOOKS YOU MAY ENJOY

Flutter	Erin E. Moulton
Journey to the River Sea	Eva Ibbotson
Keeping Safe the Stars	Sheila O'Connor
Matilda	Roald Dahl
Savvy	Ingrid Law
Scumble	Ingrid Law
The Secret Garden	Frances Hodgson Burnett
Small Persons with Wings	Ellen Booraem
Sparrow Road	Sheila O'Connor
Three Times Lucky	Sheila Turnage

Tracing Stars

erin e. moulton

PUFFIN BOOKS
An Imprint of Penguin Group (USA) Inc.

PUFFIN BOOKS
An imprint of Penguin Young Readers Group
Published by the Penguin Group
Penguin Group (USA) Inc.
375 Hudson Street
New York, New York 10014, U.S.A.

USA / Canada / UK / Ireland / Australia / New Zealand / India / South Africa / China
Penguin Books Ltd, Registered Offices: 80 Strand, London WC2R 0RL, England

For more information about the Penguin Group visit www.penguin.com

First published in the United States of America by Philomel Books,
a division of Penguin Young Readers Group, 2012
Published by Puffin Books, an imprint of Penguin Young Readers Group, 2013

THE LIBRARY OF CONGRESS HAS CATALOGED THE PHILOMEL EDITION AS FOLLOWS:
Moulton, Erin E.
Tracing stars / Erin E. Moulton.
p. cm.
Summary: During the summer before sixth grade in a small seaside town, Indie Lee
Chickory tries to follow her older sister's popularity advice by working backstage on the
upcoming community musical and not revealing that she is looking for her beloved pet
lobster and becoming friends with "loser" Owen Stone.
ISBN: 978-0-399-25696-7 (hc)
[1. Friendship—Fiction. 2. Sisters—Fiction. 3. Self-acceptance—Fiction.
4. Lost and found possessions—Fiction. 5. Theater—Fiction.]
I. Title.
PZ7.M8593Tr 2012 [Fic]—dc23
2011034396

Puffin Books ISBN 978-0-14-242653-1

Printed in the United States of America

1 3 5 7 9 10 8 6 4 2

The publisher does not have any control over and does not assume
any responsibility for author or third-party websites or their content.

For Howie, my love

Chapter 1

I DROP LOW IN THE SEAT and look out the bus window. We pass Pa's shop, Chickory and Chips Famous Fishery. I wave to the wooden pirate, Barnacle Briggs, who is always out front holding the shop sign. We zip on past and turn right onto Blue Jay Crossing. I hold my backpack on my lap. It shifts back and forth as the bus jostles over the bumpy road.

It's the last day of school. The last day of fifth grade and I'm dying for it to be over. I make a fish face in the window as we pass the harbor where Pa's boat, the *Mary Grace,* usually sits. The spot is empty 'cause he's already out making his rounds. Pa is the best fisherman in all of Plumtown and brings in the most lobsters. But that's not all. He dredges for mussels and also catches hake, fluke, flounder, monkfish, whiting, ocean perch, pollack, and sometimes wolffish. Wolffish is the ugliest fish I've ever seen, but it tastes all right if you ask me. I make the face of a wolffish in the window, pulling my mouth down into a big line from one side of my chin to the other. I pop my eyes way out and pull my eyebrows down into the middle

1

the best I can and I think it's a pretty great wolffish grin. Real menacing and gross.

"*Indie.*" I look away from my reflection and over to my older sister, Bebe, in the seat across from me. "Stop it," she says out of the corner of her mouth. She doesn't like it when I make fish faces anymore, even though she used to love it. Now she's too old and mature for that sort of thing, and whenever I do it, she pretty much pretends she doesn't know me.

I throw on a trout pout because that's the one she used to giggle at the most, but this time she groans and looks out her window.

My backpack almost slides off my lap and I grab at it. Then the bus squeals to a stop and a whole bunch of kids get on at The Manors. That's the cul-de-sac where all the rich people live. Mom says you don't move to Plumtown unless you're rich or you're a hard worker. That's the way it goes. We're in the hard-worker part. I make sure to scrunch way over in case any of the fancy kids want to have a seat, but as usual, I can spread out, 'cause three kids all cram into the seat in front of me and one sits down right next to Bebe and they start talking like they're best pals.

We go around and take a right onto Main Street, and as the breeze blows in from the open window in the seat in front of me, I can smell the mix of sugar and salt from Sandy's Saltwater Candies. I basically start drooling thinking of that delicious blue raspberry flavor. I lick my lips and consider walking home today 'cause it's about that time of year where Mrs. Callypso will be standing out with free samples. When the bus stops again, I stay scrunched over, but Lynn and June, who get on at the last stop, go by my seat and make crinkling faces.

"You stink, Indie," June says.

I can see Bebe roll her eyes across the way.

"Sorry," I say. I smell my fingers, wondering if they stink of herring from feeding The Lobster Monty Cola this morning. Herring is one of his favorite snacks. He also likes fish heads that have been sitting out for a while, and my hand might have brushed past that, too. But I don't mind if it stinks a little. The Lobster Monty Cola is my best pal besides Bebe. And even a better pal now that Bebe got all perfect and can't stand me anymore. Monty's not some ordinary crustacean; he's a golden lobster. Pa says you come across one golden lobster in every 30 million lobsters you trap. And he got Monty in a real amazing catch. Now Monty lives in a saltwater pool outside my window, and if he wants some herring and some fish heads, well, that's what he is going to get.

"Oh, seriously," Lynn says. As she passes, she pulls her shirt up over her nose. I push my hand underneath my leg, hoping that will help bury the smell.

June and Lynn sit down together over in the last seat. It's really a half seat, meant for one person, but that's where they sit. I pretend like that doesn't bother me a bit. I hum a little and look out the window and watch the joggers go up and down the boardwalk. A minute later, the brakes squeak and we're in front of Plumtown Elementary.

"Happy last day!" Mrs. McKowski says as she opens the door. Mrs. McKowski is one of the people in the hard-worker portion, too. She has driven the bus since I started in kindergarten. I swing my backpack on and stand up to get off. Every time I try to get into the line, someone else gets there first, so I wait until the very last kid has gone, then I go, too.

"See you at pickup, Indie," Mrs. McKowski says.

"Bye, Mrs. McKowski." I walk in past the giant sailor sculptures and trot along behind Bebe into Mr. Lemur's class.

Chapter 2

I WATCH THE CLOCK for most of the morning, wishing that the day would zip by just a little faster. I want to get home, relax, then go to Templeton's for ice cream. Mom and Pa bring us there every year on the very last day of school, plus days in between, but the last day of school is especially great 'cause they make Colossal Creemees for dirt cheap. That's what the sign says and that's what they do. I watch the hands on the clock tick along, thinking about what flavor I might get. Finally, lunchtime comes around and I grab a seat as quick as I can and pull out the container of lobster bisque Mom sent. The best thing about Pa being a great fisherman and owning Chickory and Chips is that we get the best meals. Mrs. Barkley works at Chickory and Chips and she makes the best lobster bisque I've ever tasted. Even though Mom develops the recipes, Mrs. Barkley runs the shop and lots of the time we have the leftovers for lunch. I unscrew the top of my thermos and pour some of the bisque into it.

A few kids pass by and I wave to Bebe, letting her know that there's a seat open right across from me if she wants it, but just as she gets up close, she veers off to the right. Marty Shanks, a kid with a mullet, sits across from me. Great. Whenever Marty sits with me, my food never tastes quite as good as it usually does. I watch a couple crumbs fall off his lips as he bites into his salami and mayonnaise sandwich, and I can't help making a monkfish face. He spots me looking at him, ducks his head down and holds his sandwich up over his mouth. Still, I can see his mangled teeth through the spaces between his fingers and they're grinding his food into mash. And between that and the cafeteria smelling like cartons of milk, my stomach gets a little choppy, like the waves before a storm.

I look over at Bebe, but the seat right next to her and the one across from her are full, so I eat my lobster bisque quickly, trying not to look at Marty. I just focus on my spoon going up and down and that's it. Then I head back to the cloakroom. As I unzip my backpack to put my lunch box away, something weird happens. My backpack shifts the teensiest little bit. I let go of it. It shifts again, and a crusher claw floats up at me from the bottom. A golden crusher claw.

"Monty!" I say, and pull the backpack open. I stare in, not believing my eyes. What is he doing here? Monty waves his claw at me and clip-claps it in front of my face. He looks like he's about to climb out. Kathy McCue comes in and I slap his claw down and step in front of my backpack so I'm between her and Monty. She goes to her fancy purple pack, then her nose starts moving up and down like a bloodhound on a scent.

"Indie Lee Chickory, you stink like the salt sea," she says, dropping her lunch box and pinching her nose. She sticks her tongue out at the same time. Well, she's not the only one who can make a stink face. I think for a minute if I want to do the puffer or the mackerel, or if I should do the pinched shrimp or the wide whale. In the end I know the trout pout is the one that will really get her. I frown, cross my eyes and suck in my cheeks. Then, for added effect, I make a groaning sound in the back of my throat. It's perfect for the job.

"Stupid weirdo," she says, and heads out of the cloakroom.

Nice work, I think as I unscrew my face and check the doorway to see if any others are coming in. It seems pretty empty, so I look back down at my pack and peer into the bottom.

"Monty Cola, how could you?" I whisper, pulling him up out of the dark and laying him across my arm. I check his forehead for dampness, because one thing I know about lobsters is that they're okay without water if they stay good and damp. But if he was in my backpack, that means he must have climbed in when I brought him the herring this morning. Which means that he's been in there

7

for a solid three hours or more. Plus, he'll have to wait until the end of the school day to get back in his pool, and that seems like forever from now.

"Not a good plan, Monty, not a good plan at all!" I say. I don't mean to be harsh, but Monty Cola thinks he can survive anything, outsmart anybody. He basically thinks he's invincible.

"Time to line up for recess!" Mr. Lemur hollers from the other room. I listen as the kids thunder toward the door. I look down at The Lobster Monty Cola and he looks at me and draws his little antennas around and around in circles.

If only I could just sneak him out and run up the street to Crawdad Beach.

"Has anyone seen Indie?" Mr. Lemur says. Dang Mr. Lemur! He's too good at keeping an eye on everyone. I crane my neck and can barely see the kids lining up at the door.

"Bebe, can you check the cloakroom?" Mr. Lemur says.

"Sure," Bebe says, real quiet. Bebe's one grade older than me, but it doesn't matter in Plumtown 'cause most of our classes are multi-age. We're in fifth/sixth with Mr. Lemur.

I turn so my arms and Monty are tucked a little bit behind my backpack. A second later Bebe walks into the cloakroom, her ponytail bouncing and her white shorts basically blinding me.

"What are you doing?" she says, flipping her silky-smooth bangs behind her ear.

"Nothing. Be right there," I say, tucking my snarly hair behind my ear with my right hand. I make an extra show of it, to keep her eyes up, not down where Monty Cola is starting to squirm around on my forearm.

I curl in, trying to hide the movement, but Bebe eyes me and just like that, she spots him. I don't know if it's his antenna or his leg or his pincher, but she spots him.

"You have got to be kidding." She crosses her arms and stalks over to me, putting on what looks a lot like a trout pout. Not that she would admit it.

"Listen—it was an accident," I say.

"What is wrong with you?" she hisses.

"He snuck into my bag," I say as Monty starts wiggling around on my arm. I pat his head, trying to calm him down a bit.

"Put him back, then," she says.

I scowl at her because she obviously doesn't care if Monty Cola lives or dies. But I can see from her jaw clenching so tight that she isn't going to let this drop.

"Is she in there, Bebe?" Mr. Lemur calls from the other room.

"Yes, coming!" we say at the same time.

"Okay, okay, I'll put him back," I whisper, and pretend like I am putting him in my backpack.

Bebe nods and then leaves. And I pull him out. Of course I'm not going to put Monty in my backpack again. I'm not some sort of heartless animal.

"I'm not leaving you here, Monty Cola. Hang tight," I whisper. I look all around the cloakroom, wondering if Mr. Lemur would notice if I have my backpack with me for recess. Probably. He's pretty smart about that sort of thing. Maybe I could make a quick escape. I look from ceiling to floor and wall to wall, but there's no window in here. I give the floor a stomp. It's really solid wood.

"That's not our best bet, Monty," I say. It would take days, maybe even years to dig us out of here. I lick my lips. C'mon, think, think.

"Indie!" Mr. Lemur says.

That's when I look down at my plaid button-up.

"All right, Monty. You've got to play dead. Got it?"

Monty lifts his pincher claw and clip-claps it twice. That usually means "yes," so I lift my shirt and push him up, then tuck the bottom of my shirt into my Carhartts so he is in a sort of pouch. I feel him curl his legs up against himself. I take a quick peek down to make sure that the buttons are not popping. It looks pretty good, pretty natural. So I saunter out into the classroom and get in line.

"All right, let's try that a little faster at the last bell, okay?"

I nod and put my eyes on the back of my sister's shiny hair as we go down the stairs. As soon as we swing out the front door and the smell of the sea comes rolling along on the breeze, Monty starts to wiggle a little.

"Hang on, Monty," I whisper. "We'll be going for a quick dunk soon."

Chapter 3

WHEN WE HIT THE EDGE of the playground, the whole line splits off—some head for the playhouse, some head for the swing set and parallel bars. I set my eyes on the farthest side of the playground. The tire swing. I walk as fast and steady as I can so I don't jog Monty up too much.

"You really do stink," Bebe says, pinching her nose and breaking off from me to a cluster of girls on the swings. I put my head down as I pass by them, but out of my peripherals I see them all pinch their noses.

"Fish freak," Kathy McCue says from the middle of them. I wait for Bebe to say something to her or push her, but she pretends like she doesn't hear. I do the same. Keep on walking. Just as I'm nearing the tire swing, June and Lynn come by and they get right in the swing so they're tucked together like two sides of an oyster shell. I veer off to the right and go over to the broad board fence that is running the length of the playground. I can easily skip over it, but doing it without being seen is going to be the trick. I walk beside it, running my fingers along the top.

I think maybe if I start listing the names of fish and crustaceans it'll give me something to do and make me look busy. "Dogfish, cusk, oilfish, hake, orange roughy," I whisper as I skip my hand over each post and land it back down. "Flounder, mountain mullet, knobbed porgy, ocean perch, pollack, sea ravens."

I scan the playground. Mr. Lemur is over at the playhouse, but he's looking around like he's on patrol, so I just keep on going. "Striped bass, yellow-striped shad, crabs, spottail pinfish, mussels, sea urchins, walleye pollack, blue angelfish."

On the tire swing, Lynn pushes off with her feet and spins in the air until she and June are looking out at me. They frown in my direction.

I get to the end of the fence and start back the other way. Mr. Lemur is facing the school now. It's just the evil pair right next to me that are jamming up my escape. Monty starts to get a little restless. I feel him flip over and his legs tickle my belly.

"Relax, Monty," I whisper. I peer over to June and Lynn again to see if they're swinging back the other way yet. But they're not—June's actually off the swing and looking at me like I'm some sort of mutant. She's coming closer, like she doesn't believe what she is seeing. Then Lynn, who is still sitting propped up on the tire swing, starts screaming and slaps her hands on her face like she's in some sort of scary movie.

"Alien!" she shouts.

At that, June stumbles backward away from me and just about every other head on the playground snaps up, scanning, like lighthouses in the night. Once they get their beams on me, there's an uproar. Hands flail and kids scream, and I start to panic, too. I fall back against the fence, feeling my face. Nothing's changed. Nose, mouth, eyes, frizzy hair. Neck is intact. It's when I look down that I see the problem. Monty's crusher claw is poking out between the buttons on my shirt, and the way he's wiggling, it looks like I have something trying to crawl out of my stomach.

"Monty," I whisper, "what are you doing?" Then I turn to June and Lynn. "Don't worry! It's not an alien."

I pull my shirt out of my Carhartts and let Monty fall onto my arm to show them it's nothing worth panicking about. But just as soon as Monty is out, he sees all the kids staring and seems to get a little stage fright, because he wiggles around in my hands. I try to grab him, but somehow he topples onto the ground. Me and Monty both freeze, standing side by side in the grass as everyone else starts to scream. Bebe crosses her arms at me and puts on an I'm Never Speaking With You Again look.

"Indie Lee Chickory!" Mr. Lemur says as he starts heading across the playground. Just as Monty sees Mr. Lemur charging, he throws both his claws in the air and starts clip-clapping them together and doing a dance on the playground. I know this dance. He does it anytime a dog tries to come up to him and anytime a cat might be nearby. One thing's for sure: He's mad. That's when everyone on the playground starts running in opposite directions. June and Lynn run away. A few boys run closer.

"Monty, stop. You're scaring them," I say, reaching down to pick him up around the middle, but he squirms away from me and continues to clip-clap.

Mr. Lemur is coming in for the kill, but just as he's getting close to me, Marty Shanks runs in front of him, trips and falls, and Mr. Lemur trips and falls right over Marty Shanks. I put my hand on the fence, about to jump over it.

"Indie, stay put!" Mr. Lemur sputters as he stumbles up. Everything is moving too fast and I'm not sure if I should go or stay.

Wwwwwwthunk!

A kickball lands next to me and bounces over onto Monty, then off into the middle of the road. Monty teeters and shivers and my heart hits my chest like it's being rammed by a great white shark. I gotta move. I don't care what Mr. Lemur says. I don't care who threw that kickball. We're under fire and we gotta get out of here.

I scoot up to Monty, who's picking himself up and wobbling to one side. I scoop him up. Then I'm over the fence and off.

As I head down Main Street, I look back, and a bunch

AS I ROUND THE FIRST BEND and head down past Templeton's ice cream shop, I hear Mr. Lemur hit the sidewalk behind me.

"Indie! What are you doing?"

But I don't even look back, and boy, am I glad I'm wearing my sneakers today instead of those fancy sandals like Bebe's wearing.

Push it, push it, push it, I think as I zip by Oceanside Players. I dodge a couple of tourists coming out of Crawdad Coffee House, but I don't see the second group that has slammed to a stop to take a picture of the coast. I run smack into one of them.

"Hey, watch out!" a lady in a jumpsuit shouts as iced coffee lands all over the sidewalk. Normally I would go and help, but not now, not with Monty injured and Mr. Lemur out to get me. I dodge tourists all the way up to Pa's store. Mrs. Barkley is sweeping the porch, and she must spot Mr. Lemur behind me somewhere, because she drops her broom.

"Indie! What are you doing?" she says as she darts

down the steps. Her bracelets jingle around her coppery wrists and her scarves dance in the breeze. They reach out for me.

"No time," I shout, running around her onto Crawdad Beach. My feet slip a little as the sand flies out from underneath my sneakers.

"Indie, stop! . . . Come back . . . to . . . school!" Mr. Lemur shouts, but I can tell from the breaks between his words that he's getting tired. I peer over my shoulder and see him falter and fall in the sand. Mrs. Barkley rushes up and helps him. Go, Go, GO, I think. And when I reach the far side of Crawdad Beach, when I reach old Mrs. Parson's land, I don't even stop, I just keep on going. Into the woods I run, quick as I can, in and out of puddles of sunlight. And the only thing that stops me is that I trip on an outcropping of rock right at the ocean's edge.

My right knee jams into the ground and my left leg wobbles, trying to keep my balance. Me and Monty look like we're ballroom dancing for a minute, the way I'm holding him up in front of me and swaying from one side to another. Finally, I regain my balance. I draw my left knee down and stop and listen, staring out at the glaring waves. My lungs are expanding so much, I feel like they're going to stretch straight out of my skin.

Mr. Lemur shouts in the distance. "Indie! Where are you?"

"You okay, Monty?" I whisper, holding him against

my right forearm and scooping some water over his head with my left hand. The water runs down the lines of his shell and pitters back to its home in the waves. Monty lifts one of his pinchers and clip-claps it just a tiny bit, but he mostly lies heavy on my arm. I settle it into the water, so he can cool off.

"I'm sorry, Monty," I say. "You should never have come to school." He wiggles a little and clip-claps both his claws, which usually means "all's well," but I'm not so sure it is. He's moving a little slow. His legs are just spinning circles in the waves. He squirms and I release him into the ocean for just a second. My hands shake, so I put my palms down on my kneecaps. I've seen Mom do this same pose before and it seems to get her calm really fast, but for some reason, I still feel hot and fuzzy all over. I peel my eyes open and pull one of my sneakers and sweat-soaked socks off. Then the other. I stick my feet in the ocean, noticing a little stinging in my calf. A thread of blood gets tugged into the waves. I run my hand down my leg. Yep, a real good bruise and a cut to go along with it.

"What the heck happened?" I say, wiggling the sting out of my toes. The words *fish freak* are ringing in my ears and I can't stop thinking about the kickball coming out of nowhere like a bomb. Pa says when you're upset, you just have to look out at the ocean and breathe with the waves. In and out, in and out. The deep breaths and the coolness of the water on my feet help my heart slow down. The wind rolls off the ocean and puts more knots in my hair, but it also seems to tug some of the energy out of me and send it off so it's not bouncing around under my skin anymore. Now I just feel like I have a rock in my chest instead of feeling like there's lightning inside.

"Indie Lee Chickory!" My calm breathing catches in my throat as I hear Mom's voice cut through the trees. She's going to be mad. I get up and jam my shoes back on as fast as I can. I reach down for Monty, and just as I do, I hear a siren go off. Officer Gallson gets bored around here, so anytime there's some sort of disturbance, he comes running for it like he thinks he's going to be a hero or something.

"C'mere, Monty," I say. "We'll go home and get you all checked out." But Monty looks nervous, and he skitters and ducks behind the rock ledge.

"C'mon, boy." I put my hand down so he can climb onto my forearm like he usually does. But instead of climbing up, he backs away slowly and hunkers down below the surface of the water.

"Monty, let's go," I say again, and this time he comes over to me, but as I reach to grab for him, Mr. Gallson's stupid siren whoops and Monty and I jump. Lobsters can drop a claw when they're spooked, and that's exactly what he does. His whole crusher claw comes off in my hand.

I scream, "Monty!" But he skitters off into the waves.

I trample in after him, holding his golden crusher. I reach down to where he went under, but a cloud of sand rises up around my feet, and when my hand gets there, it just comes up with water.

"Indie!" a voice calls from the beach.

I look around frantically, searching and searching the waves. I think I see him out toward my right, so I head that way, but as soon as I get to where I think he is, it just ends up being sun sparks on the water. I see another flash and go toward it, but when I get there, again, the gold of the sun is tricking me into thinking it's his golden yellow shell.

"Monty, come here!" I shout, getting down on my hands and knees in the water, trying to see past the reflections, but now my eyes are getting all blurry from the sun and the tears and I'm having a real hard time knowing what's what.

"There she is." That's Mr. Lemur's voice. I've made it along the waves all the way back to Crawdad Beach, and the whole gang comes rushing down to the water's edge. I bust out of the water toward Mom and Mrs. Barkley. The ocean waves fly up around my shins and ankles.

"Help!" I scream. "You gotta help! Monty got away from me. He was scared! He got away!" I hold Monty's crusher up and Mrs. Barkley takes it gently in her hand. Tears stream down my face and land like raindrops in the water, making little dents as they go.

"I can't find him," I say as Mom scoops me into a hug.

"What happened?" she says.

"He must've got into my backpack," I say, breaking from her arms and heading back into the water. "Monty!" I spit out some salt water as Mom comes into the ocean, too. "Then I thought I would bring him for a quick dunk to get cool, but he got spooked."

I look over at Officer Gallson, who just stands around looking useless, chewing his gum and putting his hands on his belt like he owns the place.

"It's all his fault!" I shout, pointing right at him. "Your siren scared him."

Mr. Gallson laughs, and I want to run at him and punch him one, but Mrs. Barkley turns me gently toward the water and we scan the whole bay, back and forth from one end of Crawdad Beach to the other. But we don't find him. We search and search until school lets out, and we still don't find him. He's in the sea. He's a golden lobster without a crusher claw. He might as well be a bull's-eye.

Chapter 5

WELL, BY THE END of the day, life is pretty much the pits. Of course, we have to hang around Crawdad Beach while Mr. Lemur tells me that I can't just go leaving school like that and Officer Gallson says I can't be making a big fiasco all around town. Then Pa comes along from the harbor and finds out I lost Monty, his grandest catch of all time.

He looks out to the sea and pulls his cap off and crinkles it between his hands.

"I'm sorry, Pa," I say.

And he reaches over and scratches my back, 'cause that's what he does to show us that everything is going to be okay. Only I can tell from his bent head and the feeling inside that it's not. Just then Bebe comes along, too, and she doesn't even talk to me. I go sit on the beach, scanning for Monty, feeling like I'm getting hammered farther and farther into the sand with every passing minute. I sit for three hours. But Monty doesn't come crawling up out of the waves.

"You ready, kiddo?" Mom asks as she comes up next to me, her bare feet skittering sand over my legs.

"Not really," I say, spinning Monty's claw in my hand.

"Well." She squats down so she's about my size. "I'm afraid Monty is gone, baby. And it's your dinnertime. He's probably enjoying his dinner, too."

She rubs my back like she's trying to press those words into my spine.

"Let's go," she says.

I stand up slow and keep my eyes on the ocean until we're all the way up Brookrun Drive to our Chickory mailbox, red and black and painted with yellow flowers wrapped around the letters in our name. Normally it's sunny and nice, but today the paint seems to be chipping and the flowers, even though they're not real, seem to be wilting. We walk down the driveway, past Mom's vegetable garden and Pa's truck loaded with lobster pots. I look away, trying to keep the tears out of my eyes.

Mom makes a garden salad and Pa fries up a couple of haddock fillets. Everything looks real nice, but I can't eat a single bite, thinking of Monty out there in the waves. I look around the table while the forks clink on our swirly-printed plates. Mom's got her yellow mug filled with lemon ginger tea. That's what she drinks when she needs to calm down. Bebe sits right across from me and eats two bites of salad and then two bites of haddock. When she sees me looking at her, she glares at me and sticks her chin out. And when I look to Pa it's the worst, because he tries to smile at me like it's some normal day.

I take a few leaves of salad and a few bites of haddock, but nothing tastes good and I just feel like I'm going to be sick, so I get up and scrape the rest into the garbage, then open the dishwasher.

The phone rings and Bebe jumps up to get it. She always likes to get the phone, which is fine with me, 'cause normally it's for her anyway.

"Hello, this is Bebe," she says, then she pauses, listening to the person on the other end. "You're kidding me!" She starts jumping up and down. I think for a split second that maybe she's so excited because someone managed to find Monty. Bebe hangs up and screams and I nearly break all the dishes, jamming the tray back into the dishwasher. I rush to her.

"What's happening?" Mom asks as she sips her tea from her yellow mug. I wait anxiously for the good news.

"I made it into *The Sound of Music*!" Bebe shouts. "At the Oceanside Players! I'm going to be Brigitta! One of the von Trapps!"

My stomach drops into my shoes. Of course. She doesn't care about Monty. This is about Bebe.

"That's wonderful, honey!" Mom says, getting up out of her chair and coming over to hug her. "I heard they're bringing in a big Broadway director for that one!"

"Yeah!" Bebe squeals. "Donald Duncan. It's going to be the best show Plumtown has ever seen."

Pa puts his glass down. "Fantastic!"

I look from one to the next, and every Chickory but me is smiling about Bebe's good news. And I think that that's just how it is. I lose Monty and make a big mess out of the whole day, and Bebe turns it right around with a great achievement. I place a honey jar, which we use as a drinking glass, into the top of the dishwasher and slide the tray in slowly.

"Can we go to Templeton's?" Bebe asks. "I can't wait to tell everyone!"

Mom stops and looks over to me. Then she rubs Bebe on the shoulder and talks quiet, as though I can't hear her. "You know what, Be, I don't think tonight's the night for that. Why don't we have sundaes here to celebrate?"

I can feel Bebe's eyes on me. Staring me down and hating me for ruining her great day.

"Okay," she says, and walks back over to the table. Her chair scrapes as she pulls it out to sit down.

Mom comes into the kitchen and gets the bowls and ice cream, and I go over and open the drawer and grab three spoons.

"Thanks, Indie," Mom says as I bring them over and set them on the table. She peels the lid off the ice cream and my stomach flip-flops.

"How many scoops, Be?" Mom says.

"Two, please."

"How about you, Indie?" Mom says.

But I can't eat ice cream tonight. Not when Monty is out in the cold ocean, alone. I have nothing to celebrate.

"I think I'm all set."

"You sure?" she asks.

"Yeah. But that's great news, Be. You're going to be famous," I say. She should be. She practices nearly twenty-four hours a day. "Um, can I watch the stars come out?" I ask quietly, looking through the window at the day turning into night.

"Sure," Mom says. "I'll check on you in fifteen."

I open the door and go onto the porch, into the quiet. I take a deep breath and try to swallow the chunk of coral that has somehow landed in my throat. I lie down and listen to the peepers begin their chorus, hear the waves roll into Crawdad Beach off in the distance. Three stars pop out of the lining of the sky and start their twinkling. After a while I hear Bebe go over to the piano and begin singing up and down. Those are called arpeggios.

"Ah, ah, ah, ah, ah," I sing quietly as I close one eye and trace the constellation Pisces with my finger. Pisces is the fish constellation, but not more specific than that. I wonder what type of fish is strung together in the sky. Is it haddock, cod, mackerel, swordfish, catfish, blowfish, trout, angelfish? Two different types of fish?

I see Mom's shadow spill onto the porch as she looks out the window at me. I guess once she's confirmed that I haven't run off, she goes back to what she was doing—probably thinking of how amazing Bebe is. I bet I could stay right here forever and they'd be delighted by their great family.

The sky is heavy with stars now, and even though we're not on an oceanfront, when the breeze kicks up, it carries a little bit of sand with it. It stings as it skitters across my skin and catches in my hair.

After a while, I hear Bebe's footsteps head upstairs and into her bedroom, but I don't feel like going in yet. I watch for shooting stars. When Bebe and I were a little younger, we'd watch the stars together, and if there was a shooter, only one of us would make the wish because we'd always end up wishing the same thing. It was only fair to take turns.

"You can have that one," I would say, and she would get a wish, and then the next time it would be the opposite. But if you had a real wish and didn't have time to wait on a shooting star, there was another way to get one. Pisces shows two fish bound together in the sky. Pa says it's our constellation, mine and Bebe's, and anyone who has a constellation can make a wish on it anytime they need to. He says it's pretty much the same as wishing on a shooting star. He even carved us two Pisces charms out of driftwood and strung them onto leather laces. We each have one.

I clasp my charm and run my fingers along the driftwood symbol. "Hello, Al Rischa," I say to Pisces' brightest star, pointing at her with my other hand. I trace the fish across the sky over and over. One side to the other. I pretend I'm dipping my hand into the dark the way I dip my hand into the ocean. I drag it down through the universe, pretending I can spin the stars in my path into circles and pinwheels. I picture them bending away like seaweed as my hand nears them. I trace Pisces from one star in the constellation to the next, to the next, to the last. And back again. I watch for a long time. I think about losing Monty, Pa feeling sad about it, Mom having to listen to Officer Gallson, Bebe getting embarrassed on the bus and on the playground. I think of Kathy McCue pinching her nose and calling me fish freak. And I think of Monty, wounded in the waves. I squeeze my eyes closed, take a deep breath and make my wish.

"Please, Pisces, promise . . ."

I think of the best way to say it so it's clear to her. "Promise to make me a better Indie Lee Chickory."

That sounds right. I run my thumb along my charm and send the wish up into the sky. I want to be a Chickory who could make Mom and Pa and Bebe smile. A Chickory who could find The Lobster Monty Cola. A really good Chickory, not the fish freak of Plumtown.

Chapter 6

EACH MORNING FOR THREE days, I jump out of bed and run down to Crawdad Beach, looking for Monty. I even send Pa with a few photos of Monty to show to the other lobstermen in case he gets caught in one of their pots, but every day when he comes home, nothing. No sign of Monty anywhere. I had set out a couple of fish heads in the sun on that first day, and by today, they're really cooking up good and strong.

"Going to look for Monty!" I say to Mom as I head out across the yard with them.

"Indie!" Mom stands up from her spot in the garden, tossing a few green beans into her bowl. I stop. "Kiddo, I think he's long gone by now."

"Maybe," I say, turning back toward Crawdad Beach.

"Don't get your hopes up is all I'm saying!" She wipes her arm across her forehead.

"Okay!" I shout, skipping into a run.

"Oh, hey, wait!" she says.

I stop, groaning.

"Since you're going that way, will you grab lunch from

Mrs. Barkley and bring it down to Bebe at Oceanside? She forgot hers. Lunch is at noon."

"Okay!" I say, tying the fish heads to my belt. I head across Main Street and onto Crawdad Beach. I duck into the trees. It's cooler here. The woods are double green with pine and elm and maples. The canopy blows gently in the sea breeze, and flickering sun sparks dance between the leaves. I walk for a few yards, then hop over a downed tree. I veer to the right so I am hugging the coastline. When I get to the rocks where I lost Monty, I sit down and peel off my shoes. I splash my feet into the water and dig my toes down deep, so far that I can feel the ocean's heartbeat in the soles of my feet as the cold water splashes up around my calves.

"Come from the sea, Monty," I sing quietly, not loud and proud like Bebe would, but it's still not bad.

I watch the waves roll in and splash. I watch for his tail, his pinchers waving, his antennas spinning circles in the waves. But nothing. I untie the fish heads from my belt loop. They're smelling good and ripe, just the way Monty likes them and Bebe hates them. I pull some string out of my pocket, lean back and tie one end onto a twig. Then I tie the other end around the tab that's holding the fish heads together. I spin them so they're not gawking at me while I fix the knot, then I drop them into the ocean so they bob on the waves.

"Monty," I call. "Where are you, boy?"

I sit and wait for a minute, keeping my eyes peeled on the glaring bright ocean. A few baitfish come up for a snack, and one crab, too. I pull my toes out of the sand to make room. He skitters away at the mini earthquake.

"Yeah, you better move on. This is for Monty!" I shout, then I quiet down because I know my voice will carry all the way to town on this breeze and Officer Gallson will probably think he needs to be some hero, come running to save a kid from getting lost in the woods. Pa says Officer Gallson is starved for things to do.

"C'mon, Monty," I say, but the truth of the matter is, I'm cursing myself for not coming last night. Monty and most other lobsters move around and get their meals during the nighttime. When it's dark, they're more active. Still, maybe there's a little cave he went into in the rocks here. I step into the water, brushing past the fish heads, which are all slimy now that they're soaked up again. I walk out along the wooded coast, away from Crawdad Beach. I watch the rock ledge, but there doesn't seem to be a good little cave for Monty anywhere along here. As the water becomes deeper, I step back up onto the rock shelf. I push past a pine bough.

And stop dead in my tracks.

Not 'cause I see The Lobster Monty Cola, but because just where the rock shelf folds into the dirt of the woods, there's a tree house about fifteen feet up off the ground.

It's crumpled in on itself and one window peers out past the deadwood. I shiver, watching half of a ladder swing in the sea breeze a few feet in front of me. It looks spooky swinging there, like a hanging man.

Still, I lick my lips and turn out toward the ocean and back. Maybe it would be a good lookout when I come back tonight to see if Monty's going to come after the fish heads. Yeah, it might be a real good lookout. I step over to the ladder and reach up, seeing if I can touch the bottom rung, but my fingers land about a foot underneath it. I jump, extending my fingers, but as I do, the Center Town Chapel bell rings. I land back down and listen. I count the bells, hoping they end at eleven. But just after eleven comes one last bell. It's noon already? Bebe's lunch! I rush back toward the ocean, jump in and run along toward the fish heads, rinsing the fish stink off my hands as I go. When I reach the fish heads, they're all still there, bouncing in the waves. No luck yet. Maybe Monty'll come by while I'm gone.

I leave 'em, jump up and run out toward Crawdad Beach.

Push it, push it, push it, I think as I head to Chickory and Chips. I reach Main Street and dodge in front of a few slow-moving cars whose passengers are taking their own sweet time looking out at the coast. I bound up the steps past Barnacle Briggs and bust through the door. The bell jingles and jangles behind me. Like Mrs. Barkley knew I'd be coming, she already has a canister of clam chowder in her hand and passes it to me as I run up.

"You better go, kiddo. It's already after noon!" Mrs. Barkley says, her neck scarves blowing in the breeze from the open window.

"Thanks!" I say. I barely stop to grab ahold of it. I just snap it up, take a spoon and a napkin from the counter display, spin and run down toward Oceanside Players. Hoping I'll be on time.

Chapter 7

I HURRY UP THE SIDEWALK to the Oceanside Players and onto the flower-lined pathway, filled with color and sweet smells of geraniums and foxgloves. I roll to a stop, my eyes landing on a beautiful red rosebush at the far end. The last time I was in the middle of the Oceanside Players yard was with Bebe. We'd ended up here by accident.

Mrs. Barkley and Mom were testing out a Thai green curry mussels recipe. I remember Bebe and me standing in Chickory and Chips, watching the lobsters scuttle around in the live tank and doing a fish-face challenge in the glass.

I made a blue marlin face and Bebe giggled. "That's a six out of ten. Try this on for size." She sucked her cheeks in, frowned and tilted her head down like she had a big long forehead.

"The Atlantic croaker," I said, tracing the reflection of her face on the tank glass.

She jumped up and down. "You could tell what it is! That's double the points!"

Then I busted out laughing 'cause no one really cared how many points we got, we just cared how funny it was. It's impossible not to smile when someone throws you a fish face. Well, not totally impossible, but pretty near impossible.

"Girls," Mom said, and we both looked up from the tank. "I need you two to run down to the docks. Your father, Kilroy or Denty must have some mussels. We've run out and we're not done tinkering."

Bebe and I set out toward the docks, looking for Pa, Mr. Kilroy or Mrs. Denty. We got through probably fifteen fish faces on the way down. I pulled out the tautog, the triple tail, the oilfish and the sand perch. Bebe did a bunch also. She had a catfish going, using her fingers as the whiskers, the cutlass fish and the wahoo. We were having a great time. We passed Sandy's Saltwater Candies and kept on going down Main Street. Oceanside Players had a big old sign out front that read ACTORS GALA, 4 PM. I didn't think a thing of it on the way down and I only noticed it because Bebe sang the sign to me.

Eventually, we reached the docks and ran along down the wooden planks. The first boat we came up on was the Muddy Mollusk. That's Mrs. Denty's boat.

"Mrs. Denty!" we hollered, waving and jumping down the dock.

"Well, hello, girls," Mrs. Denty said, setting down a bushel basket on the deck of her boat.

"Mom and Mrs. Barkley are looking for some mussels," I said. "They're working on a recipe and they're all out."

Mrs. Denty took off her cap and put it under her left arm. "Well, I got some mussels," she said, raising her right arm and kissing her biceps. Mrs. Denty is always good for a few jokes. After we all stopped laughing, she took one of the baskets and started shoveling some mussels into a paper bag for us.

"Got a couple of good pulls today," she said, filling it to the top. "Some starfish in the dredge, cramping my style, but not too bad." She handed us the mussels. "I'll settle up with your old man when he gets in."

"Thanks!" we said, and headed out. Bebe carried the bag, elbowing me when I tried to take it.

"I've got muscles, too," she said, and I didn't argue with her 'cause I didn't mind Bebe doing all the work if she wanted to.

We made our way back toward town, making fish faces and laughing all the way. That's until we reached Oceanside, of course. It was already past four o'clock now and the whole lawn was set out with tables and white tablecloths and lovely trays and racks with lots of pretty-looking foods. There were even flower petals spread out on the tablecloths. And in front of and around the tables, there were ladies with dresses that were lovely and long enough to kiss the grass, and men in black and white suits with bow ties and important-looking puffy chests. I started wondering about the flowers, about who picked all the petals off, but then I realized Bebe wasn't walking by with me. I looked back, and sure enough, she'd slowed to a stop and was gazing at the whole scene like it was a beautiful dream.

"Bebe?" I said, walking back to her.

She sucked one of her cheeks in, but it seemed like she hardly heard me. I followed her gaze out across the lawn. And sure enough, there was a girl about our age, between seven and eight. Not old at all, someone you wouldn't even imagine could be in a play. She and a few of her friends were dressed up all fancy. They looked just like miniature adults, or like the bride and groom figurines you see on the top of wedding cakes. The little girl went up to a microphone that was set out on the veranda and tapped it twice. Then she started singing like an angel. And like she was the Pied Piper or something, Bebe started walking toward her. It seemed as if the girl sent out a line and was towing Bebe in.

"Bebe, what are you doing?" I said as a few old couples looked our way. But she didn't answer me. She just moved forward with a half-fish, half-starstruck look on her face.

I stepped around a cloth-covered chair with some pink ribbons on it and kept right alongside her.

Before long, Bebe and me were standing in the middle of the fancy-dressed people in nothing but our crummy T-shirts, shorts and sandals. I started noticing the sand between my toes and on my legs from being at the beach that morning. We *were sticking out like sore thumbs, but I didn't want to leave Bebe and run home.*

The little girl sang like a star. She raised her arm up in the air, her perfect mouth becoming an O as she hit the final note. She lowered her hand as she lowered her voice and I was pretty impressed, too, about how nice it was.

"Wow," Bebe whispered as everyone around us started clapping.

The girl bowed and stepped right down the stairs. Just then, Bebe rushed forward. Well, that caught the little girl off guard, I guess, and she screamed and put her hands over her mouth, and that caught Bebe off guard and she fell, the bag of mussels ripping open and spilling all over the little girl's beautiful satiny dress.

My hand shot right up to my mouth and Bebe popped out of her daydream fast.

"Get those disgusting things off of me!" the little girl screeched, curling her toes away from a few mussels that had landed on the ground.

"They won't hurt you," Bebe said, scooping up a handful and trying to put them back in the ripped bag.

Some people in the crowd rushed away and some rushed forward; some bent down to help. As Bebe and I looked up, the little girl put her pretty satiny glove up to her nose and pinched it.

"This stinks. My night is ruined. Thanks a lot."

She said it straight at Bebe. Then stormed away, to the

side of the theater. Bebe's hands froze and she dropped the
last mussels onto the ground. Her mouth was hanging open
like a lost guppy.

"Be?" I said, putting some mussels back in the bag.
But Bebe turned and she ran.

A quiet little sniffle pulls me from my memory and my
head snaps up. I get that twisting feeling in the pit of my
stomach. It's a same-blood, same-bones type of ache, the
kind you get when you know your very own sister is feeling sore and you can feel it, too, without a word passing
between you. I step over to the edge of the pathway and
look down the side of the building. Sure enough, curled
up in the shade against the wall is Bebe. I head across the
grass toward her. Bebe is wearing her Pink Ladies jacket
from the musical *Grease* and her hair is up in a perfect
ponytail. Not one single strand is out of place.

"Be?" I say, going up to her real slow so I don't startle
her. She lifts her head, looking at me, tears slipping down
her cheeks. But at the same time as she looks sad, she
looks really mad. Her tears cross the crinkles her face is
making as she grabs the canister of clam chowder out of
my hand and tears the lid off of it.

I gulp and dig around in my pocket for the spoon.
When I pull it out, I see it's cracked in half from the run
I made down Main Street, but the scoop part is still

intact. I swallow, sorry that I'm ruining this meal on top of everything else. Maybe she won't notice.

"Here you go," I say. She takes the half spoon out of my hand and scowls at me like I did it on purpose. Then she starts crying all over, like I punched her in the stomach rather than gave her a bad spoon. She makes all sorts of noises and my chest starts feeling real hollow. Like our two feelings are connected through the air, I feel like crying, too. I shift my feet in the sand, wondering how to make her feel better, but nothing comes to mind fast enough.

"Where were you?" she says, digging into the clam chowder. "It's almost twelve thirty."

I look down at my feet and make a wounded-mackerel face. Not on purpose, but just because that's the type of feeling that's going on inside, so that's what comes out.

"Stop," Bebe says. "Please?"

I jerk my head up. "What?"

Bebe rolls her eyes. "I've been hiding back here for twenty-five minutes." She sniffles, standing up. A little bit of the creamy chowder falls down onto her Pink Ladies jacket. I look at the spill. I pull a napkin out of my pocket and wipe at the collar, but she swats my hand away and pulls the jacket off.

"It'll wash out," I say.

But she goes over to the garbage can that's standing next to a door marked STAGE and tosses it in.

"There'll still be a stain," she says. "If I hadn't been rushing—"

"Sorry," I say, really meaning it. "I didn't mean to be late."

Just then we hear laughter bubbling through the summer air. I look up and there's a group of kids walking down the walkway. Bebe grabs my shoulder and we both press ourselves flat against the side of the building.

"Be quiet. I think they'll go through the front door," she says.

I zip my lips but keep peering that way. There's a girl out front who is about Bebe's age, only she's dressed like a movie star. She has a fancy billowy shirt and she's wearing sunglasses that almost cover her whole face. The kids disappear onto the veranda and I hear the front door creak open.

"Who is it?" I whisper. "Why are we hiding?" Wondering if this is the gala incident all over again.

"It's Kelsey Duncan. The director's daughter," Bebe says, stepping away from the wall.

"So why are you hiding from her?" I say, stepping out, too.

Bebe looks at me like I'm some sort of idiot. Like I should know who this girl is and why we would be pressed up against the wall trying to avoid her.

"Listen—getting a lead in a play is all about networking."

"Networking?" I say.

She rolls her eyes and takes another bite of chowder.

"If I'm in with her, I have a better shot. My name might come up at dinner, or when they're talking about the next big production. You know, *networking*. It's all about who you know."

I shrug, wondering if she read this on one of her acting blogs. "But if you want to network with her, then why didn't you want her to see you? Why do we have to hide?"

"Because," she says, "they all went to the tables over at Templeton's with their lunches. What was I going to do, go empty-handed? Look like the real poor kid out of the bunch? I told them I was going to meet some of my friends from school."

"But—"

"I don't want her knowing that I've just been sitting here by myself, crying the whole time. That looks even more lame than not having any food at all."

On the word *lame,* she takes the last bite of chowder and shoves the empty canister into the garbage can. She turns back to the stage door and opens it.

"I'll see you later," she says. "Sorry, but it's just, could you do something . . . right for a change?"

"Sorry," I say again, feeling like there are sand crabs scurrying around inside my stomach.

She steps inside, the door closing softly behind her. I stare at it for a minute, thinking. Bebe's not trying to be mean; she just needs everything to be perfect. I put my hand up to my Pisces charm. No wishes coming true yet. Maybe the star didn't hear me.

The door swings on its hinges the teensiest bit and I can't help but open it a little and look inside.

Bebe's in the middle of the stage, past a few big drapes. She looks tiny out there.

"Great, let's begin at the top," a voice says from the audience.

The kids all line up, and Bebe smiles at a boy next to her, who smiles back. Then they step into some choreography. Mom and Pa would be so proud if they saw her. That's when it occurs to me. Maybe I should try doing something less like Indie and more like Bebe. Maybe that's the key to being a better Indie Lee Chickory.

A man with a headset and a clipboard comes by and stops when he sees me.

"May I help you?" he asks, pulling the door closed behind me, bumping me into the theater.

"Uh . . ." My tongue sticks in my mouth. But he looks at me and then down at his watch and I figure if I want to do this, I better make it good. "I'd like to sign up for the play," I say, shuffling my feet.

He smiles. "Sorry, kiddo, auditions are closed."

"Oh." I turn toward the door.

"But if you want to help out, they could always use some people downstairs."

"Downstairs?"

He points toward a dark stairwell. "Check in with Mr. Bluesey."

"Oh, thanks," I say, walking in that direction. I make my way down to a big metal door with a sign that says SCENE SHOP, PROPS, LIGHTS, COSTUMES. I lick my lips and put my hand up to it. At least it's something in the theater, right? It's definitely something Indie Lee Chickory wouldn't normally do.

I push it open.

"Yes?" A man with a bushy white beard looks up from a drafting table.

Don't jam this up, I think. I try and find my words. "Uh, I heard you could use some help, uh, in the, uh"—I look back at the door to the first sign—"the scene shop," I say, shoving my hands way into the pockets of my Carhartts. I step in farther and the door closes behind me.

He looks me up and down.

"Well, you're certainly dressed right for the job." He glances back down at the drafting table, flips his pencil over and starts erasing. "The scene shop, though?"

I nod. "Oh yes. I've always wanted to work in the scene shop," I say, thinking I'm doing a great job at sounding sincere.

The old man nods. "I have to admit I'm a little surprised. But hey, that's fine. Sloth's way in the back. She's solo because everyone else is afraid of her, so there's plenty of room to help. That's for sure."

My heart drops like a rock in the waves. Oh great. I turn and look down the hall.

"Yep, that's the way. Go down past the costume shop, past props, keep on heading past the lighting graveyard and you'll find her there. Can't miss her."

I take a step, but one of my feet just doesn't want to move.

"Well, do you want to help or not?"

"Oh yes," I say out loud. "Just . . . uh . . . past the graveyard?" I feel my insides turn to mush at the word. Walk past the graveyard to the scariest person down here? Great plan, Indie.

"Yeah, you'll see the lights," he says, going back to his work.

"Tha-thank you," I answer. Then I concentrate real hard on putting one foot in front of the other.

Chapter 8

AS I MAKE MY WAY down the hall, I'm thinking that this is just about the weirdest place I've ever seen. The first door I come to leads to a room filled with costumes. There are racks of shoes and hats, and three walls are lined with hanging pants, suits and dresses. A lady with pretty brown hair that's pinned up in a French twist smiles at me as she pulls a needle from between her teeth and secures it into a fold of fabric on the mannequin in front of her. Why didn't I say costume shop?

I turn back and the old man, Mr. Bluesey, just points past me. I hear music in the distance. A thump underneath my feet. I keep on walking. The hallway is plastered with posters from plays and musicals past: *Seussical, Cabaret, Mary Poppins, Arsenic and Old Lace, West Side Story, Pirates of Penzance*. Signatures are caked on everything.

I look in the next door and there is a slightly older lady sitting in the middle of the office in front of a desk that is piled with odds and ends. Above the desk are more shelves covered in fake flowers, canes, vases, clocks, framed paintings. The sign on the door says WELCOME TO PROPS. ENTER

IF YOU DARE. The older lady lifts her dust rag off the grandfather clock she is polishing and waves at me. A kid with freckles, thick-framed glasses and hair like straw pops up from behind a pile of suitcases.

"I think this'll do nicely for Maria's trip to the von Trapps. Don't you, Aunt Peg?" he says in a nasally voice.

"That'll work great, Owen," she answers.

When the Owen kid spots me, he drops the suitcase and tilts his head to one side. I duck out of the doorway and keep on going. I know I'm getting closer as the thumping gets louder and louder, the smell of sawdust stronger. There's a big opening to my left where a bunch of what I'm guessing are stage lights stand one beside the other, like row upon row of robots. A guy with long hair peeks out from the dark and then another one comes up on the right.

"I need a lens for a thirty-six degree, four C-clamps, and let's salvage all the safeties."

"You got it, Tommy," guy one says, while Tommy checks off items on the clipboard in front of him. Besides the fact that they're speaking their own language, they seem nice, too. Guy one waves, dumps a couple of items in a bin, and both he and Tommy wheel it down the hallway.

That's the graveyard, I guess. And just past that, the hallway ends. One door in front of me. And it's closed. I stare at it for a minute. Then take a deep breath and put my hand on the knob. A saw screams and the thumping of the music won't quit. I feel it against my palm. I turn my hand, push the door open a tiny crack and peer in. The music rolls out like thunder and almost bowls me over.

Oh boy.

There in front of me is a skeleton-skinny girl, maybe in high school. She's wearing all black and what looks like a dog collar around her neck. She's got tattoos up and down each arm and her hair is gelled up in five sharp-looking spikes. She could probably murder someone just with those. Even scarier is that right in front of her is a big saw. She lifts a lever and lowers it, sending a piece of wood flying out the side and into a bin at the end.

"Sloth is of the punk persuasion."

I jump back against the wall and stifle a scream. The kid with the glasses, Owen, is standing in front of me. He pulls a leather-bound book out of his back pocket. He unrolls it in his hand and I can see the cover is floppy and worn. He starts flipping through the pages. Then he turns the book toward me, points to a small scribbled paragraph and starts reading. "Punk is a subculture that threatens the norm. Punks wear clothes and listen to music that fit their subculture. Sloth is also a vegan, someone who doesn't eat meat or animal produc—"

Before he can finish, the door flies out of my hand and Sloth is standing there looking at both of us. She has so many face rings, she looks like a fish that never gets caught but just drags the hooks away into the deep blue sea.

"May I help you?" she asks.

Owen slams his book shut and disappears like a guppy from between a shark's teeth. I stare, trying to think what to say. And Sloth stares at me. Straight into my eyes like she can see my soul. The music dies down and for a minute there is an awkward silence while we just frown at each other. As the next song begins, Sloth starts to move her head back and forth to the rhythm of the music, faster and faster. Then she screams in my face and I freeze, thinking maybe if I don't move, she won't see me or she'll forget I'm here or something. I freeze so good, I don't even breathe. She breaks away from me, swinging and head-banging all around the shop. And the third time around, she grabs ahold of my wrists and pulls me in.

I feel stiff as a dead fish, but try and nod to show her how great it is and how I don't want to get axed. Finally, she gives up and just shakes her head.

"Lamesauce. What do you want, anyway?" she says.

I try and pull my voice up from my stomach, but it's not moving.

"Well?" She turns the music down a little. As it fades, I relax the teensiest bit.

"I'm here to help," I say.

"Okay," she says, picking up a tool belt and tossing it into my hands. "Can you paint?"

I nod.

"Can you hammer?"

I nod again.

"Are you attuned to fine details?" she says as she picks up a huge wrench and holds it over her head.

I jump back and shield my face. She laughs as the end of the wrench lowers behind her head and she starts scratching her back with it. I take a deep breath and uncurl.

"Yes," I say. Of course I'm attuned to fine details. Just look at how many fish I can tell apart. I can even tell the difference between every different type of grouper. There's the black grouper, the Nassau grouper, the yellowfin grouper. I can also tell the females from the males.

Sloth nods toward a pile of wood on the floor.

"Throw that in the scrap bin and then I'll find something else for you to do."

I go over to the scraps and start picking up the pieces of wood. I watch for Sloth over my shoulder, keeping one eye on her the whole time. Sure, being in the theater might be all around a good idea, but somehow I feel like I've made a big mistake.

Chapter 9

IT'S A PRETTY ROUGH couple of hours. Mostly, Sloth has me carry things here and there and fetch things for her. It's just one loud song after another on the iPod dock and I'm thinking about Monty most of the time. But I suffer along, and when five o'clock rolls around, I go to the stairs and bust up them to find Bebe. I check the stage and don't see anyone there, so I head through the auditorium to the front door, down the steps and up the path to Main Street. I spot Bebe up ahead, walking alone, and I dodge around runners and bikers and joggers until I get near her.

"Bebe!" I shout, coming up next to her. She holds her script against her chest and almost drops it when she sees me.

"Oh, hi," she says.

"Guess what," I say.

"What," Bebe says, looking over her shoulder like she's afraid to be walking with me.

We pass Mrs. Callypso handing out Sandy's samples. I grab a blue raz one off the tray and Mrs. Callypso smiles at me 'cause she knows that I already know what those candies taste like, but she doesn't mind me taking one all that much.

"I'm going to be helping out in the play!" I say, shoving the taffy in my mouth.

Bebe stops in her tracks and I run right into her while trying to dodge an oncoming lady with a fanny pack.

"What?" She says the word so it stops short at the *t*.

"I'm going to be helping out with the play. Down in the scene shop," I tell her.

I expect her to put her hand on my shoulder and tell me that I've done something right for once. But instead of doing that, her shoulders slump down into a frown and she starts running up the road toward Chickory and Chips and Brookrun Drive.

"Be?" I say, running after her.

When I reach her, she's turning onto our road.

"What the heck's the matter?" I ask. "I thought you'd be happy. You're always talking about how embarrassing I am. This'll help make me better."

She glares at me out of the corner of her eye and keeps a fast pace all the way up to the house. We scoot down the driveway and up the steps. The whole way, I wait for her to say something. When we get inside, Mom is pouring some iced tea, and as we come through the door, she spills a little on the counter.

"Indie, where in the devil have you been?" she asks. "I

thought you were going to come back for lunch. You've been gone for hours without telling anyone where you were—"

"She's been at the shop," Bebe spits.

Mom, confused, looks from me to Bebe and back. "No, she hasn't. I checked in with Mrs. Barkley."

"Not *that* shop," Bebe says. "The scene shop. Indie got it into her head that she should help with the play."

"Oh!" Mom tips the pitcher again, fills an empty honey jar with iced tea and hands it to me. "Well, that's a great idea!"

There. My heart bounces like two dolphins jumping. Someone appreciates what I'm trying to do. I take the iced tea.

"It's *not* a great idea," Bebe says, going over to the piano and setting her script down on it. "The theater is mine. I don't want Indie around. She's—" She looks me up and down, and I try to smooth my hair a little. "She's just going to embarrass me."

"Don't be hurtful," Mom says.

I drink the iced tea, not realizing how thirsty working in the scene shop has made me.

"I think it's a great idea," Mom says, grabbing a towel out of the drawer in front of her. She places the dripping iced tea pitcher on top of it.

Pa walks in and I move away from the door. He peels off his boots and sets them on the shoe rack.

"Guess what, hon!" Mom says. "Indie's helping out in the play. Both our girls are going to be busy at Oceanside Players this summer."

Pa smiles a genuine smile, just like he did when he heard that Bebe was in the play the other night. It's the first genuine smile I've seen for three days.

"That sounds great." He comes over and squeezes my shoulder, and I look at Bebe, waiting for and wanting her approval. But she kicks off her flip-flops and storms upstairs to her room.

Chapter 10

BEBE AND I DON'T SAY much at dinner. Not to Mom and Pa and not to each other. After, I go to my room and look out at Monty's saltwater bath that's sitting outside my window. I stand on my tiptoes to check the dome and the tunnels to see if maybe Monty decided to take a hike up Brookrun and come home. But there's no sign of my golden lobster friend. I slump over and lean my head down on my desk.

I'll have to bring a bait bag filled with herring. Monty might be in the mood for that instead of the fish heads I brought today. As I push back my desk chair, a knock comes at the door. I open it. Bebe.

"What do you want?" I ask.

She takes my hand and drags me up to her room. She closes the door and crosses her arms, standing in front of it.

"Well, since you're going to be in the play, and since everyone is going to know that you're my sister"—she takes a deep breath like she can't believe she's saying it—

"you at least have to act the part. Okay? I'm going to give you a makeover."

I can't believe it. This means she's actually going to accept me in. This means my plan to be in the play might just work.

"I can do that. I can play the part," I say, reaching up and rubbing my Pisces charm. I sit down on the bed and push Mrs. Kitty, a gigantic stuffed tiger, over so I can lean up against the wall. I watch Bebe's eyes follow Mrs. Kitty. Bebe hates it when I move anything in her room, but I guess the makeover is more important, because she clasps her hands. "All right," she says. "Where to start?"

I just shrug, not knowing.

"First off, we need to do something with your hair. Are you trying to grow dreadlocks?" She grabs her pink hairbrush from its spot on her bureau.

"No, I'm not trying to grow dreads," I say, even though I like dreads. Mrs. Barkley has black dreads with silver streaks in them and it looks magical. But I know Bebe doesn't like her hair even the teensiest bit snarly. She crams herself between the wall and me, pushing me to the edge of the bed with her knees.

"Gentl—ow!" I say as she digs into a snarl and yanks the brush straight down. My eyes fill with tears and my nose feels stingy.

"Hold Mrs. Kitty, then. We have a lot of snarls to work

out here," she says, putting the tiger into my arms and digging in again. Like holding a stuffed tiger is going to help when I feel like I have nails being driven into my scalp.

"You're killing me!" I say, grabbing a piece of hair near the root. The piercing feeling disappears a little bit as I hold the hair. It doesn't ease up enough for me to ignore it, but it does ease enough for me to at least stop myself from crying. I hold Mrs. Kitty with one hand and hold my hair with the other until about thirty minutes later, when she works through the last knot.

"Better already," Bebe says as she parts my hair down the middle. She pulls two elastics off the end of her hairbrush and I stare at the posters on her wall as she puts my hair into two French braids. Everything in here is so pink, I feel like I'm in Barbie's playhouse. And on the walls there are pictures of all of Bebe's favorite shows. *High School Musical*, *The 25th Annual Putnam County Spelling Bee*, *Grease*.

Bebe scoots around me and goes back over to the bureau. She puts the hairbrush down and angles it sideways so it's just the way it was when I came in. Then she picks up a handheld mirror.

"Improvements, right?" she says, holding it out to me. I take it and look in it. I look a little like one of the girls from down at The Manors. I definitely don't look like myself. I do a quick puffer fish to see if I can get her to smile, but she yanks the mirror out of my hand and gives me a warning glare.

"Do *not*," she says. "This is a no-fish-face zone."

I swallow and my cheeks deflate. Bebe turns back to the bureau and the room fills up with music as she opens her *Phantom of the Opera* jewelry box.

"Earrings," she says, pulling out two pink dangly ones.

"Nah," I say. "I don't think I need those. I don't even think the holes are still there." I feel my earlobe with my thumb and index finger.

"They're right there. They take forever to close up. Didn't you just wear earrings for Mom's birthday party last month?" she says, holding the earrings up to each side of my face and looking them over.

"Yeah, but—"

She puts the pink pair back, picks up some blue circular ones, closes the box and bounces onto the bed. I feel a tiny pinch as she pushes an earring through.

"Bebe," I say, trying to dodge her as she moves to the other side.

"Stop," she says as she grabs my other earlobe and puts an earring in that one, too.

"My whole head feels like it's on fire," I say, squishing my face with my fingertips.

"This is nothing compared to the primping we have to do to get ready for a show," she says, like that's supposed to make me feel better. Then she jumps off the bed and opens the bottom drawer of her bureau.

"You need to lose the Carhartts," she says.

"I like my Carhartts," I say, putting the tiger down. "They're comfy and useful."

"You look like a boy. Even that shirt. It's . . ." She looks at me, thinking of the right word. "Well, it's just boyish."

"It's comfortable," I say.

She digs around in the bottom drawer, pulls out a pair of bedazzled jeans and holds them up to me.

"No way," I say.

She nods and smiles over the top of them.

"No," I say, thinking about what Sloth is going to say when I walk in tomorrow. She's definitely going to smash me with the pipe wrench if I wear those. That gives me an idea. "I'm going to be painting and gluing and getting wood shavings everywhere. I better stick with my Carhartts. I don't want to ruin your clothes."

Bebe takes a look at the jeans and puts them back in the drawer, and for a minute I think I've won the battle. But then she pulls out a pair of regular blue jeans.

"These are cute ones. And"—she holds up a finger—"I have the perfect top."

She lays the jeans on the floor and riffles through her T-shirt drawer.

"You can change into those," she says as she searches.

I slide off the bed and take off my Carhartts. At least I'm not stuck with the studded ones. I can make the regular jeans work. And since Sloth has a tool belt, I won't be needing a hammer loop. I pull the jeans on and Bebe hands me a black shirt with CATS written across the front of it. I take the shirt and slide out of my plaid button-up.

"Great," I say.

But now Bebe's in her closet and not listening to me a bit. She's humming one of the songs from the show. I recognize it but can't quite place the tune. As I neaten the shirt and fold my other one, Bebe spins and puts a black scarf around my neck.

"Wow," she says, dragging me over to the doorway, where there is a full-length mirror hanging from the door frame.

I look at myself. I look just like Bebe. A little bit darker with the black shirt and the black scarf. Not as much pink, but still, pretty much like her.

"Now, tomorrow, just be casual. Collected," Bebe says. "The bonus now is that we're both *in*." She uses air quotations on the word *in*.

"What's that mean?" I ask.

"We're both *in* the theater. That's major. Kelsey says theater people are special. Talented."

I examine myself in the mirror, straightening some hair that is already puffing out of one of the neat braids Bebe made.

"Tomorrow, we're going to try to get in with Kelsey. I'll do the talking. You just follow my lead."

I nod, hoping I can perform under pressure.

"Networking, got it," I say.

She smiles and goes over to her alarm clock. "Be ready at seven thirty sharp."

I watch as the digital numbers flip and turn until they say five thirty.

"Wait, five thirty or seven thirty?" I say.

"Oh, must have made a mistake." Bebe clicks the buttons. The numbers flip again until it says 7:00 A.M.

"Don't be late!" Bebe says. Then she goes over to her bureau. I back toward the door as she starts singing softly to herself. She neatens the scarf she has laid out on the top of the bureau for decoration. Then she rearranges the items on the top like she's assembling a shop window. She walks over and readjusts Mrs. Kitty.

"Night, Be, love you," I say, opening the door and going out.

"Night! Love you!" she says.

I head downstairs and go straight into my room. Mom and Pa are busy watching TV shows.

"Mom, can I go and check to see if Monty is there?" I holler. "He's probably out hunting now that it's dark."

"Absolutely not," Mom says. "It's eight thirty at night!"

"Pa?" I say.

"Listen to your mother. Besides, there's a very narrow chance that Monty will ever be caught again. A golden lobster's one in every thirty million. He's a very rare catch."

"Okay," I say real quiet as I open my bottom drawer and throw my Carhartts in with all the others.

I close the door, walk over to my desk and look out at the saltwater pool. I keep seeing my reflection in the glass and keep thinking it's Bebe, not me, so I grab my plaid button-up and put it on over the CATS shirt. Then I unwind the scarf from my neck and put it over the back of my desk chair. Just for now. I pull Bebe's earrings out and put them on the bureau so I'll remember them in the morning. I open my window and lean on the sill, letting the cool breeze wash over my face. That's when I realize how easy it would be to jump out. I'm on the ground floor, after all. It's just a small little jump down and I'd be out of here.

My hands are working before I even know it.

"Indie, you all right in there?" Pa hollers as the screen hits the outside of the house.

"Okay," I holler back. "Just dropped my book. I'm going to read and go to bed. Night!"

"Night!" Mom and Pa say.

I jump up into the window and step out, feeling the soft grass under my bare feet. I grab the bait bag that's still sitting in the dome in Monty's saltwater pool. I squeeze it, feeling through the mesh. There's a few squishy spots and a few hard bulby areas. It's still filled with herring and a couple of mollusks. I head down to Crawdad Beach. I'll just check on him real quick and be back in a jiffy. It'll be so fast. No one will know.

Chapter 11

I HEAD ACROSS THE LAWN, trying to be like a shadow in the night. Once I get out of view of the house, I book it down Brookrun Drive straight to Main Street and across the sand, into Mrs. Parson's land.

I duck into the trees. It's much darker here with the branches holding hands overhead. It's like they're playing Red Rover with the moonbeams and only a couple are getting through. I go quiet as I can, not wanting to spook Monty if he's been here, and not wanting to spook myself with my footsteps crunching through the leaves. Halfway there, I feel something crawly on my arm and smack it off as fast as I can. Then I think I hear something just behind me.

"Who's there?" I turn and look, but I don't see a thing.

"Monty, is that you?" I whisper, continuing, one slow step at a time. I swallow hard and tell myself to relax. I listen to the waves come rushing in and take a few deep breaths with them and go over my fish names alphabetically to distract myself.

"Anchovy, black grouper, bar jack, cod, crevalle jack,

cutlass fish." I pass through the trees to the rock outcropping and step out into the silvery moonlight. I see the moonbeams surfing on the waves and the fish heads bouncing around, and that makes me feel a little bit better. At least I can see in front of me.

I get up to the water's edge and stick my feet in, then reach down and pick up the string and pull in the fish heads. They skitter up onto the rock as I pull, and I can't believe what I'm seeing. There's actually a whole head missing. At least most of a head is missing. I pick it up and lean so my shadow isn't over it, so I can see by the moonlight. And sure enough, the marks on it look just like lobster marks. I see a dent where Monty would have grabbed ahold of the fish head to hold it still. Then he would have worked his way down the fish's face. I've seen him eat a fish head like this a million times from my window. This exact pattern. I lick my lips, scanning the waves. No guaranteeing it was Monty, but it sure could have been.

"Monty," I say out toward the ocean. "I've got some herring, boy!"

A little skittering noise skips around in the trees to my left. I turn, trying to see past the shadows.

"Monty, is that you?"

I squint but it doesn't help at all. All I can see are shadows, leaves and rocks. The sound comes again. I put down the bait bag and the fish heads and follow the scritch scratch through the trees. I push past the pine bough to where that old abandoned tree house is standing, and my voice catches in my throat as the ladder swings in the moonlight. I run my tongue across my lips 'cause it feels like all of a sudden my whole mouth is filled with sand.

"Butterfish, round scad, scaled sardine," I whisper, trying to remain calm. "Chub mackerel, carp, kelp." I jam up 'cause kelp doesn't sound right. Sounds like seaweed rather than fish. A shuffling noise comes again, and I think it's coming from somewhere near the tree house.

"Hello?" I say.

"Hello?" says a quiet voice.

I jump backward about ten feet and my heart lurches into my throat. I search the shadows and the tree house, but there's nothing there. Nothing talking to me. I reach down and feel around the ground for a rock. My hand finally finds one and I grasp it in my fist.

"Who's there?" I make my voice as big as I can. Turns out it isn't that big.

Whir-whur—there's a mechanical noise, like something that would be attached to a robot or an alien, and a second later a branch just past the tree house starts to shake. I pull back the rock and aim. The trees shake again and out comes a pair of glowing beady little eyes.

"I'm not giving up without a fight!" I say. I throw the rock as hard as I can and turn to run the other way.

"Ow! Why?" I stop dead in my tracks and spin slowly back around. A boy steps out into the moonlight. He pulls a set of goggles up so they're on top of his head, and he readjusts his glasses. Then he pulls a handkerchief out of his pocket. "Another bloody nose."

It's the kid from the theater. Owen. I put my hands on my hips.

"You scared me half to death. What are you even doing out here?"

"I might ask you the same thing." He goes up to the ocean's edge, leans down and starts splashing his face with the water.

"I was checking on my lobster," I say, "to see if he'd come and eaten any of the food I left him."

"Your lobster?" he says. "Say, that's funny. I'm checking on a lobster, too." He puts the kerchief to his nose and pinches it.

I step back then, wondering what the heck this kid is doing here, at this spot, in this town, at this time of night, checking on a lobster.

"I heard an aurum *Homarus Americanus* escaped the other day around these parts, and I wanted to see if I could spot him."

"A what?" I say, recognizing the *Homarus Americanus* as the scientific name for lobster. "What's *aurum*?" I'm afraid I might already know the answer.

Owen pulls the handkerchief away from his nose and looks in it, but then I guess he decides that his nose isn't done bleeding, 'cause he puts it back right away.

"That means 'gold.' A golden American lobster escaped. Did you know they're one in every thirty million?" he says, pinching his nose still, so his voice is even more nasally than it was this morning.

"Yes, I know it's one in every thirty million." I cross my arms. "And for your information, that's my lobster. I'm the one who lost him. His name is Monty."

Owen pulls the handkerchief away from his nose and stares at me with wide eyes.

"Wow, can I help you find him? I'm great at searching, and look!" He pulls the goggles off his head and hands them to me.

I take them and spin them in my hand. They look like any ordinary pair of spectacles, but then there's another set of thick lenses you can pull down over the top of them.

"What are these?" I ask, trying to cool off a little.

Owen checks his handkerchief one more time. "All better," he says, and pulls a book from his back pocket. He unrolls it, and I realize it's the same one he was showing me earlier today when he mentioned that Sloth was "of the punk persuasion." He flips through, the pages fighting him in the breeze. Finally, he opens the book and lays it flat out on the rock. I step into the moonlight and we both kneel down over the page.

"I'm going to have these patented," he says, pointing.
Dual night-vision and magnification goggles
Underneath it is a diagram with lots of labels and

arrows. It looks a little like the drawings in the scene shop.

"They're modified night-vision goggles. It's an original work. See, if you flip this switch here"—he takes the goggles from my hand and flips a little switch on the side—"you have the magnification lens as well as night-vision goggles. Or"—he flips it again—"you can have the option of one or the other."

"Wow," I say, not really meaning it. The truth is this Owen kid seems kind of nice, but he sure talks a lot, and I don't want him spooking Monty so he loses his only remaining claw. I wonder if my fish faces will work on him like they do on Kathy McCue. I switch my face from wounded mackerel to flat haddock to trout pout to see if anything might scare him off.

"Say, are you practicing for something? You've got some interesting expressions. May I ask your name?" Owen says.

Hrm. Not working like it usually does. Probably due to those braids that Bebe put in my hair. I undo my face so it's back to normal. "Indie Lee Chickory."

"I'm Owen Stone," he says. "I just moved here from Oak Ridge."

"How do you like it?" I say, 'cause that's something I've heard Bebe say to someone else who had just moved here.

"Well, to be honest . . ." He sits down and wraps his

arm around his knee like he's settling in for a story. "I hate it here. As far as I have observed, it's about two degrees too hot. There are loads of my least-favorite insects, black flies, probably due to the humidity, and I've been tucked away helping Aunt Peg with props, so I've made exactly one friend, yourself. Plus, I am becoming vitamin D deficient from being stuck inside all day. So far, life in Plumtown is the pits."

I flick my right ring finger with my thumb. Then I hear a little splash off in the distance and I lurch to my feet.

"Monty?" I say. There's more skittering, splashing and scraping.

"Here!" Owen says, handing me the goggles.

I take them real quick, without even thinking, and put them on. Both lenses lowered, I look down the rocks, and even though the lenses make everything in my vision yellowy green, I swear I see a lobster tail kick into the waves. It nearly fills the lenses, it's magnified so well. I pan back and forth.

I see a little ripple in the waves as the fish head gets pulled away. When I scan back, the last fish head pops to the surface. A green eyeless face. I pull the goggles off.

"Was it him?" Owen says. I hand the goggles back.

"I think it might have been. Thanks," I say. My heart beats through my whole torso, telling me everything is going to be okay. "I just have to catch him."

"How?" Owen says. "By luring him in?"

"Yeah," I say. "I'll have to set up a post here. I'm sure he'll come once he knows it's me looking for him."

I look back at the dingy tree house. If I could just get rid of all the broken boards, it would make a perfect post. I reach up to the ladder again, trying to stretch with all my might.

Owen comes over and reaches his hand way up, too.

"It's approximately eight inches from my reach." He goes over to his book and starts writing some notes. I see him nod and chew his cheek in the moonlight. "You know, if we got rid of all the scrap boards and just had a platform, it would provide good viewing of nearly the whole bay. Additionally, we could set up the bait right out front, here."

"Why do you keep saying 'we'?" I say.

Owen looks from me to his book to the fort and out to the ocean.

"I mean, if you'll have my help, that is. You can use my night-vision goggles. I can help in any way. I promise I'll be an invaluable resource."

I think about it for a minute.

"But you're not going to keep him. He's my lobster."

Owen nods. "I'd really like to meet him. That's all. I don't have to keep him."

"All right," I say. "You can help. *If* I can use your magnification goggles."

"Oh yes, I have even better equipment that I can bring tomorrow night. You'll see."

The watch on Owen's wrist beeps. "I guess I'd better go. I'll see you tomorrow, then." He places his goggles on his head and goes toward the trees. I wait until he disappears behind the leaves. Then I look out into the night and spot Pisces. I hold my necklace.

"Thanks, Al Rischa," I say into the sky. 'Cause already I'm on the way to finding The Lobster Monty Cola and to being a better Chickory.

Chapter 12

"INDIE, YOU UP?!" Bebe hollers. My eyes are fighting me to stay closed, like the top lashes are giving the bottom lashes a big bear hug.

I manage to tug my eyelids apart at the same time that she barges through my bedroom door.

"Why aren't you up?" she says, flipping the light on. "We need to be there early if we're going to get a chance to talk to Kelsey."

I rub my eyes and sit up, taking my water glass and slurping some down. My eyes unblur as I suck down the water and I see Bebe chewing the nail on her thumb, then index finger, then thumb.

"Uh," Bebe says, "you look like a codfish."

I take one last swallow and then slide out of bed.

"Must have overslept," I say.

"I thought you went to bed early." She's looking at my jeans and shirt, which are hanging off the back of the chair. "How'd you already get these dirty?" she asks, noticing the cuffs on the bottom of the blue jeans. I watch as she holds a pant leg and starts brushing the dirt off. Think fast, Indie.

"I don't know. I—I just came right down here after leaving your room," I tell her.

"Only you can get dirt everywhere when there isn't even any dirt," she says, giving it one final smack and then rushing out the door. "Hurry, hurry, hurry!"

I get up, jump into the jeans, throw on the shirt and the scarf and go into the bathroom. I close the door and start brushing my teeth, but a second later, Bebe's in here, too.

She's got the brush in her hand again.

"Restless sleeper much," she says, pulling the bands off the ends of my braids. She unwinds them, combs them out and re-braids them as I spit in the sink and rinse my toothbrush.

She twists the last band into place, double-checks herself in the mirror, then grabs a little perfume spray bottle and spritzes it above my head.

She takes a deep breath. "There, much better," she says.

I blink my eyes fast 'cause, despite smelling like roses, it sure stings my eyes.

We head toward the kitchen. I grab my sneakers and shove my right foot in.

"Oh no, sorry, not those ratty things. Here." Bebe drops

a nice pair of strappy sandals in front of me. I peel my sneaker off and put the sandals on.

"Mom, we're heading out!" Bebe calls.

"Leaving already?" Mom says, looking up from the pantry. She pulls her pair of gardening gloves out and slides them on. Mom works in the garden all day, every day.

"Yeah!" Bebe says.

"All right, well, don't forget your lunches."

"Okay!" we say together as we each grab the prepped haddock Tupperware sitting on the counter and head out the door.

As we hit Main Street, I smile thinking about being out there last night and seeing Monty in the ocean. We wave to Mrs. Barkley as we pass Chickory and Chips, then head past Sandy's Saltwater Candies. When we get up to the Crawdad Coffee House, Bebe grabs my arm and we both press up against the side of the brick building.

"There's Kelsey and Mr. Duncan right there," Bebe says, breathing heavy and pointing.

I look through the shiny coffee shop window. It's the movie-star girl again, only this time she has a sweater vest on and a ridiculous-looking skirt. Her gigantic sunglasses are up on top of her head. And her buckled shoes are so shiny, they're nearly blinding me.

"The sand is going to ruin those shoes within a week," I say.

"Shh," Bebe says, still gripping my arm. When I look again, they're headed toward the door. Bebe pulls me into the little pathway between Sandy's and the coffee house. She holds her finger up to her lips. I look over her shoulder and watch some blue saltwater taffy spin on the stretcher in Sandy's. My stomach growls.

"Shh," Bebe says again, like I can control my stomach growling. Still, I put my hand over it just to tell it to relax a little.

"Why are we hiding?" I whisper.

Bebe peers around the corner and gives me a nod that says we can move out.

"We don't want to show up before them," she says. "We'll look too eager. Trust me."

We step back onto the sidewalk and follow them. Bebe shuffles along slower than usual. We watch Kelsey and her dad go down the flower-lined pathway, up the steps and into Oceanside Players. Bebe slows her pace even more.

"Just remember—I'll do most of the talking. And please, please, please do not make any fish faces. Okay?"

"Yeah, yeah, I got it," I say.

"Promise," she says, reaching for her Pisces charm.

"Pisces promise," I say, reaching for mine.

She tucks a loose strand behind my ear and nods approval. We take a right onto the walkway and head up the stairs into the playhouse. It's like Bebe has planned every step. As we push the big oak door open, I spot Kelsey next to the ticket counter with one of the older von Trapp boys. Bebe walks right up to them. I walk closely behind her.

"Morning, Ian," Bebe says to the boy.

"Hey, Bebe," he says.

Kelsey turns and looks at Bebe and then me. Her eyebrows go up. I run my tongue across my teeth and think about looking normal.

"Kelsey." Bebe cradles her score against her chest. "This is my sister, Indie. She's working backstage."

Kelsey doesn't smile but puts out her hand. I uncurl my fist from my pocket and shake it real fast.

"Hi," I say, looking to Bebe to see if that was too much or not enough. She gives me a smile.

"Hi," Kelsey says.

"So," Bebe says, "I was practicing the thunderstorm scene last night and, well, Indie actually suggested that you might be able to help me with it?"

I can feel Kelsey's eyes move from Bebe to me, and I relax my face to be sure I am not making any fish faces. I dig my hands into the pockets of the jeans. They're not as roomy as my Carhartts, but they'll have to do.

"She heard you rehearsing yesterday when she came up from the scene shop and was saying how great you were," Bebe says.

"Yeah," I say, "really great."

Bebe gives me a warning glance, so I seal my lips and nod at her.

It must work.

"I'd love to help you," Kelsey says, cupping her hands together like she's holding a dove and bringing it to her heart. It looks more like a gesture you would do onstage than in real life. "My dad said they're starting at the top, with Maria and the nuns. But you and I can go run lines and practice, maybe backstage or outside?"

"Oh, thanks so much," Bebe says. She's using her stage voice, not her genuine Bebe voice. But Kelsey sure seems to like it.

They walk through the auditorium and up the stage steps. I follow along. Just as we reach the wings, I see the stage door swing open. In comes Sloth. She's got earbuds plugged in, she's wearing high-top sneakers and she's sporting a spiky collar around her neck. Bebe and Kelsey jump back about three feet. Sloth doesn't look at anyone, just bolts down the stairs and out of sight.

Kelsey puts her back to the door and pushes it open. "Are you working with her?" she asks, looking at me. I look over at Bebe to see if I should go ahead and answer this, and she gives me a nod.

"Yeah," I tell her.

"Good luck!" she says, staring down the stairs to where Sloth's disappearing through the door.

"Thanks."

Bebe smiles at me as they swing outside. "See you later, sis." She gives me a thumbs-up and I give her one back. I feel my Pisces charm bounce against my chest as I walk down the steps, and it gives me a warm feeling right where it lands, *boomboomboom,* right on my heart.

Chapter 13

WHEN I REACH THE SHOP, the music is blasting out of the speakers again. I walk in quietly, go over to the corner and pick up the tool belt that Sloth let me use yesterday. She nods as she studies a floor plan that's laid out on the shop floor. I nod back at her and give a little half smile. She gives me a once-over. Then she goes over, flips off the music and comes and stands in front of me. She looks from my earrings to my scarf to my braids and all the way down to my toes. Her nostrils flare and her nose ring twitches. I take a little step back as the good feeling I had coming down here burns out in the pit of my stomach.

"Morn—"

She puts her hand up, chopping my word off mid-sentence. I swallow it back down.

"What is wrong with this picture?" she says, waving her hand toward me like she's a magician.

I reach up and pull the blue earrings out of my ears. Sloth shakes her head and sucks in her cheeks, making a big sigh like she's trying to keep her patience but has to concentrate on it really hard. She continues to glare.

"Not the earrings?"

She shakes her head. Of course not the earrings, Indie, I think. She has five actual fishhooks in each ear this morning.

"My scarf?" I say quietly. Her nostrils flare and my heartbeat somehow makes its way to my palms and toes.

"Well, that's a start. Could get sucked into a power tool, but that's not what I'm getting at." She looks straight down and puts her hand on her chin.

"Oh, my shoes?" I say.

"Ding, ding, ding!" she says, sticking her neck out and swinging her hand in the air like she's ringing an invisible bell.

"My sist—" I start to explain, but Sloth puts her hand in front of me and snaps her fingers closed like a fish snapping on bait.

"Zip it. I don't care about who stole what from who. Got it? You need to go home and get your sneakers."

"Bebe says—"

"I don't care what Bebe says. Who's Bebe, anyway?" Sloth goes back over to the floor plan. I look down at my hands to see if they're shaking as bad as I think they are. Yep. I dig them into my pockets.

"Does Bebe know anything about shop safety?" she asks.

"No," I say, my voice a lot quieter than I mean it to be.

"Huh?" She's looking up at me.

"No," I say again, making sure I'm louder this time.

"Does Bebe know that Frank Shawsheen once dropped a set corner on his toe and severed it right off because he was foolish enough to wear sandals to the shop?"

My toes curl as far under my feet as the sandals will allow them to go, and my voice seems to be somewhere in my shoes, too.

"Well? Does she?" Sloth says.

I lick my lips. "No."

"So?" Sloth looks at me. And it's like her gaze pushes me toward the door. She starts nodding. "Yes, that's the way. Don't come back unless you're planning on wearing your sneakers. Safety first in my shop."

"Okay," I say. "Okay, I'll— I'll be right—"

Sloth goes over to the iPod dock and turns the music up. It fills the air all the way into the hallway and drowns out my voice completely.

"Be right back," I say, turning to go.

"Seriously, on the day I need the most help—" I hear a board hit something solid and am glad I'm not still there. About three feet back toward Mr. Bluesey's office, I need to take a quick break against the wall and catch my breath. If I just run home and grab my sneakers, I can throw them on in the shop and then switch them when we leave. I head toward the door.

"Hey, Indie, is that you?" Owen hollers as I pass by props. I stop and look in. "Where you going?"

"Just home to get my sneakers," I say, rubbing my hand across my forehead. "I, uh, I forgot them."

"Can I come along?"

I shrug without realizing it.

"Great! Aunt Peg, can I go along? It'll just be a minute and I'd really like to see the town a little bit more."

Aunt Peg looks over the tops of her glasses at me. "Sure," she says. "Nice to see you talking to someone your own age, anyway. Come straight back, though, okay? No detours."

"No detours!" Owen says as he grabs his book off the props desk, rolls it up and puts it in his back pocket. Then he tucks a pencil behind his ear and hurtles out into the hallway. We head up the stairs and out the stage door.

Chapter 14

IT'S NOT UNTIL WE'RE in the blazing-hot sun that I realize that just ten minutes before, Bebe and Kelsey went out that same door. I'm blinded for a minute as we move from the dark of the theater to the sunny day. And I shield my face, hoping beyond hope that somehow they don't recognize me. But then I hear them up toward the front of the building and realize I'm safe. I won't have to play fifty questions with Bebe. I blink the sun out of my eyes and listen.

"Raindrops on roses and whiskers on kittens," Bebe sings.

"Very good, but a little bit more from the gut and a little bit less from the nose. Think nightingale, not nerd; think Garbo, not geek."

"Oh, okay," Bebe says.

I follow the sound of their voices until I've spotted them up ahead, on the veranda. I can see Bebe's back from here. Owen heads straight for the main road. Straight up the building. Straight toward them.

"Owen," I hiss. He stops and turns. I gesture toward the bushes.

"What?" He raises his palms to the sky.

"Shortcut," I say, pointing toward the hedges that run alongside the lawn of the Oceanside Players. If we go this way, Bebe won't see me leave or return and she won't be mad I'm switching out her pretty sandals for my ratty sneakers.

Owen smiles and comes back over to me.

"Oh, I had no idea," he says as we duck underneath a branch. I squeeze through to the other side. Owen follows me. We walk out to Main Street, keeping the hedges between us and the porch.

"Do you know I've mapped out every possible escape route from my aunt's house?" he says.

"No, I didn't know that," I answer quietly.

"It's always a good idea to know your exit strategies."

I walk, looking at my feet, until we get to Templeton's. Then I hurry up the sidewalk, but Owen is taking his own sweet time. He goes over to Squiggles' fish stand and stares at Mr. Squiggles.

"May I help you, son?" Mr. Squiggles says, his thick mustache moving up and down.

"How hot do you have to have the oil to make the fried calamari?" Owen pulls the pencil out from behind his ear.

"Owen, we gotta go," I tell him. "No detours."

But Owen starts making notes about the calamari.

He even touches a piece with the eraser of his pencil. Mr. Squiggles' mustache begins to twitch. He's much more serious than some of the other shopkeepers. Mrs. Barkley's nice as can be and Mrs. Callypso is always giving away free candy. But Mr. Squiggles says that a businessman can't be giving away freebies all the time. "Would you like to *buy* something?" he says.

"Oh, no, thanks," Owen says. "I'm mostly interested in your methods."

Mr. Squiggles does not like the sound of that, I don't think, because he puts his hands on his hips and stares at Owen.

"No detours," I say, grabbing Owen's arm. "Sorry, Mr. Squiggles!"

He glares at Owen as we walk away.

Owen reluctantly puts his pencil back behind his ear and follows me down the sidewalk.

"What a serious fellow," Owen says as we walk past Sandy's. He stares in at the taffy, which I know he can't help. I stare at it for a minute, too.

"Listen, we gotta keep moving," I tell him, shaking my head.

And this time he falls into step beside me, his hay-like hair bouncing lightly in the breeze. He takes a deep breath.

"Did you happen to see the sunrise this morning? It was beautiful over the ocean. Very red."

"Red sky at night, sailors' delight; red sky at morning, sailors take warning," I say, thinking of Pa.

"What's that?" Owen asks.

I drop my hand and look over at him, not believing my ears. "You've never heard that?" I say. "Red sky at night, sailors' delight? Red sky at morning, sailors take warning?"

Owen shakes his head. "Must be some colloquial jargon found primarily in coastal towns. This is my first coastal town. I've previously only been an inlander."

I shake the drop-jawed guppy look off my face as we take a left onto Brookrun Drive.

"Are you a robot or something?" I say.

"No, I'm just left-brained," Owen says, shrugging. "My, there's some nice foliage along this road."

We get to the tree line before my yard.

"Here we are," I say.

"If you don't mind, I'll do a few leaf rubbings while you're getting your sneakers."

"Sure!" I say as I see Owen bend down and pluck a fern. "I'll be right back."

I jet out across the lawn and inside.

"Hey, kiddo. Everything okay?" Mom says from the kitchen sink. She has a whole bunch of carrots that she's scouring in a colander.

"Just forgot my sneakers," I say, grabbing them from their spot near the door. "I can't be in the shop without my sneakers."

"Oh, that makes good sense." Mom places a few of the washed carrots onto a paper towel next to the sink.

"See you later!" I say, heading back out the door. When I get to Owen, he's just pressing his book closed.

"Is that your diary or something?" I ask, pushing off my sandals and shoving my sneakers on. Owen stands up and adjusts his glasses higher on his nose. I tie my shoes, then grab the sandals, and we head toward town.

"A diary? Of course not," he says. "I don't own a diary."

He holds it out in front of me. The faded brown cover is scribbled on with marker: *Owen's Book of Logic and Reason: Observation Log IV.*

"Looks like a diary to me," I say.

"Like it says, it's a book of observation . . . and reason."

"So, a diary with a fancy name?" I say as we hit Main Street.

"No, this is like a lab book. Scientists use them to document trials and errors of their experiments, only mine has that plus general observations of the universe, important facts and efficient and executable plans."

I just look at him.

"Like Edison. You ever heard of him? Once he was a full-time inventor, he kept a notebook as a record of his inventions and activity. He spawned great works from what seemed to be random scribbling. Da Vinci, too. You ever heard of da Vinci?"

This kid is nuts, I think.

"You have heard of them, right? Edison? Lightbulb? Da Vinci? *Mona Lisa?*"

"Yes, I've heard of them!" I say. "So it's not a diary. Got it."

Owen trips as we pass Chickory and Chips. His foot catches right on the step and he careens over, his book skittering across the sidewalk. Mrs. Barkley is out the door as quick as can be.

"Oh my, are you all right, darling?" she says as she helps Owen up. I go to his book and retrieve it from the sidewalk. When I lean down, it's open to a page. I don't really mean to look, but I can't help it. All the marks around the side. Doodles of his inventions. And lists, too—they catch my eyes.

> *Innovation X: Glassesbook*
> *Observation XI: Plumtown: quiet, dull*
> *Innovation XI: Leaf Evaporator*
> *Observation XII: Relapse*
> *Stats: 12 pm, yelling, door slam. 12:10 gone.*
> *Innovation XII: Robot Dad*

"Indie?" Mrs. Barkley says as she hands Owen his glasses. "Were you going to introduce me to your friend?"

Owen puts his glasses on and blinks a few times. I press his book shut.

"This is Owen," I say, handing him the book. "He's new here."

"Hello, ma'am. Thank you very much for your kindness," Owen says, then turns to me. "You ready?"

"Yeah," I say, and we head down Main Street, back to the playhouse and inside.

I think Sloth feels a little bit better about my outfit, but she doesn't mention it a whole lot. I place the sandals by the door and drop the scarf on them, too, 'cause I don't want anything getting caught up in a saw or power tool. She grunts at me and hands me a list of things to do. I paint a few smaller set pieces, then she hands me a broom and a Shop-Vac and points toward the floor, so I clean stuff. I sweep the big chunks and vacuum the small ones, and think on Monty and how we're going to bust down the boards of that tree fort tonight and have a great lookout. I peer over at Sloth's shelf filled with tools, and I look at the tool belt she gave me that's equipped with a hammer, some pliers, a little pocket filled with screws and another with nails. It would be perfect to bring along.

"Pack it up!" Sloth says at the end of the day. I take my time putting the broom away in the corner and she throws on her backpack, puts her earbuds in and heads out the door. I'm afraid of just taking it, but more afraid of asking permission. So I wait until it's really quiet, then I tuck the tool belt into a burlap bag by the corner and toss it over my shoulder. As I go to the door, I spot another hammer, lying there. I grab it and jam it into the bag. I push my sneakers off one at a time and put the sandals back on. Then I tuck the sneakers into the bag as well. Lastly, I wrap the scarf back around my neck and head up the stairs and into the theater. Just as I duck out the stage door, Bebe grabs my arm.

"It worked like a charm," Bebe says. She spins me into a hug. I try and keep the bag behind me, but she still notices it. "What's that?" she says.

"Nothing. Just stuff that Sloth wanted me to bring home to work on."

She raises her eyebrows and looks toward the veranda. Then shrugs. "Everyone's gone now, but in the long term, that bag has got to go. I'll give you a new one in the morning."

"Okay," I say, relieved. We start walking.

"Kelsey *and* Mr. Duncan said that I have a beautiful voice, *and* that I'm really getting to know the choreography. If I keep this up, I'm going to get a great part in next summer's production. I just know it."

Bebe sings as we walk down Main Street. And I feel pretty good, like if I had a solid voice, I would pitch in, too.

"It's going to be the best summer yet," she says, linking arms with me as we head down our driveway and make our way up the stairs and in the front door.

Mom looks up from the kitchen counter, where she's mincing garlic and onions and throwing them into an already-sizzling pot.

"Hey, Mom," Bebe sings.

"How'd it go?" she asks, spinning a carrot and slicing off the end.

"It went great," Bebe says, turning and slapping me five. I meet her in the middle.

"My, it's nice seeing my girls getting along so well." Mom smiles at us. I go into my room and drop the bag out my window.

"Dinner's ready in thirty!" Mom says. I sit down at my desk and watch the saltwater pool, thinking of Bebe's smile and the thumbs-up she gave me. Thinking of Mom noticing how great Bebe and I are getting along. Thinking of the bag of tools from the shop and how we're going to use them to make the best lookout for Monty. I breathe in, and the onions and garlic cooking on the stove make my tummy feel warm, like the ocean on a sunny day. It's all coming together.

Chapter 15

IT'S DARK IN THE TREES. I make sure the tool belt is fastened tight around my waist. Then I stand on the milk crate that Owen has placed underneath the ladder and I jump. I manage to grab the third rung, and from there I can latch my feet onto the bottom one. The ladder seems sturdy enough, I think as I climb up to the branch. I sit on it first, then lean against the trunk and stand. I place my feet like I'm on a balance beam, one foot in front of the other, except I use the limb above me to make sure I don't fall.

Owen climbs next, and a second later he and I are standing on the branch together. He turns his flashlight toward the open window. And we both step over to have a peek at what's inside. There's no raccoon or squirrels or thousands of bats as I'd expected. But there's something that tells my feet to run and jump and get home to bed. Twinkling like snow in the sun is the biggest spiderweb I've seen in my entire life.

"Disgusting," I say.

"Fascinating," Owen says.

"I am not going in there," I say.

"It looks like they're primarily cobwebs, not active webs." He says it like it's supposed to make me feel better.

"So what," I say.

"So, there're probably not that many arachnids in there."

"You can't tell," I say, snapping a small branch from the tree.

"Still, it's a shame to have to destroy a habitat. But we can't leave it there, so I'm in agreement with your plan."

I take a deep breath and put the branch through the window, then I spin it like a cone in the cotton-candy machine. The webs break and turn and wrap around the leaves and branches. Owen keeps the light straight on the scene, watching for spiders to come scurrying out. I reach the branch into just about every corner, then I toss it over the edge as fast and as far from me as I can get it.

Owen goes in first and I stay back for a minute, trying to see if I have spiders climbing all over me. It sure feels like I do.

"All right," Owen says through the window. "All clear! Where should we start?"

I grab on to a broken board and use it to help me get onto the platform. I step over a few downed shingles and go over to Owen. That's when I really see the damage. Half a roof, sagging walls, shingles and dirt everywhere.

"I guess we should just junk everything and keep the platform," I say. "That'll be the best way to see the ocean."

So we get going. Owen tucks his flashlight in one of the trees so we can see our work. We kick and hammer and knock things off the side. Good boards go off the right and bad boards go off the left. We push the entire half of the roof off and it crumples in a heap to the ground. And the last bits of wall come away with squeaking nails and cracking wood. And just like that, we're on a platform in the trees. I take a deep breath and look out at the ocean. From here, we're a few feet in from the sea and about fifteen feet up, so when the waves rush in, it looks like we're sailing out under the stars.

"Cool," I say.

"What a marvelous illusion," Owen says.

I scan the waves for the dips and spins of a lobster tail. But I don't see too much.

"I brought some professional equipment," Owen tells me as he climbs back down the ladder and retrieves his backpack from a tree branch. Then he climbs back up and pulls out what looks like different parts of a telescope and starts putting them together.

As Owen clips pieces into place, I stuff a new bait bag with two ripe fish heads that I grabbed from Pa's muck bucket. That's the bucket he puts gross fish stuff in when he's gutting and filleting them.

I crinkle my nose, thinking about how much Bebe would hate the smell right now.

"Do you think this stinks?" I say, putting the fish head up toward Owen's nose.

Owen screws the top of the telescope onto the tripod base and looks at me like I'm a two-headed lobster.

"Of course it stinks," Owen says. "The natural metabolic process that the fish is undergoing during its decay is giving off trimethylamine oxide."

Well, that's about as opposite from Bebe as you can get. "But it doesn't bother you?" I say.

Owen shrugs. "No, not really."

I tie a piece of string onto the fish's jawbone as Owen peers through his telescope. "Hey, shooting star!"

I look up fast but miss it.

"We see them a lot here," I say. "You can have it."

"I can have what?" he says.

"You can make a wish," I say.

"No, thanks," he says, peering through some more.

"What? Why?" I scan the sky, watching for another one.

"Don't believe what they tell you. About wishing on shooting stars," Owen says.

"What do you mean?" I ask, finding Pisces in the sky.

"I mean, if life is crummy, don't expect life to be great because you wished on a shooting star. It's just a meteoroid meeting the Earth's atmosphere. It burns up when it hits, creating that tail. There's nothing magical about it. It's science."

"Okay, thanks, Mr. Spock," I say, thinking about Pa's favorite movie.

"I'm just saying, superstitions like that may make people feel better in the short term, but they have no real grounding in reality."

"Maybe so," I say, "but when you've got nothing to lose, what's it hurt to wish on a few shooting stars?"

Owen shrugs and spins the telescope so it looks straight up through the trees, then flips his book open to a dog-eared page that says *Observation X: Time to Initiate Self-Improvement Plan.*

I try not to look at the page real long 'cause anything that says "self-improvement plan" seems kind of important and, well, personal. I secure the line attached to the fish head onto the tree limb in front of me and throw it down into the ocean. When I look to see if Owen is done writing, I can't help but catch a glimpse of his page again.

Wish on more shooting stars.

I guess I'm not the only one who needs work, I think as I jiggle the rope a little, hoping the head will draw Monty's attention. I find it kind of reassuring, somehow, that Owen has something he's working on, too.

Chapter 16

"YOU WANT TO TAKE A LOOK?" Owen asks as he closes his book and peers through the telescope. "I figured we could use some real magnification, made by professionals, to spot Monty." He swings the telescope out toward the open ocean.

"Sure." I stand and put my eye up to the telescope. I spin it down below the tree house, then out into the open ocean and back again. I do this a few times. Way out, I think I see a dolphin jump. But when I keep the telescope there, nothing else happens.

I let go.

"What if he never comes back?" I say, clunking down onto the platform.

Owen leans up to the eyepiece and looks through. "I think we have to get into his head more. I haven't done much research, but I'd imagine that lobsters are driven more by routine or instinct than emotion."

"What?" I say. Monty is the most emotional lobster I know. Still, I hear Owen out 'cause he seems to be pretty smart and prepared.

"I mean, think about it. Your dad didn't catch him because Monty wanted to go and live with humans or anything. He caught him like any other lobster."

I think for a minute.

"Well, not exactly like any other lobster," I say. There were a few specifics about it.

"What do you mean?" Owen asks, opening his book to a blank page and licking the tip of his pencil. He looks up at me like he's ready to listen to a history lesson.

I sit down facing the ocean and swing my legs over the edge of the platform in case Monty comes along. This way I'll see him. I think back on how Pa always tells the story of the catch of the great golden lobster.

"It wasn't some ordinary day," I say. "Pa dropped his lobster pots on the day he got his brand-new boat. The *Blue Bandit* was out of commission, bad motor or something, and Pa managed to sell parts of the boat and save up for a brand-new one, the *Mary Grace*. Pa said he knew the *Mary Grace* was a special boat to begin with because me and Bebe suggested the name, after Mom.

"The first morning with the *Mary Grace,* he dropped his lobster pots, and when he got to the last pot, he noticed that he was out of bait bags. Also, the lobster pot was worse for wear, missing a bit of the webbing. He was sure that he wouldn't catch anything in it but decided to throw a couple of fish heads from his muck bucket inside and toss it overboard all the same. Just as he was throwing the pot, he reached for his Coke to grab a sip and he knocked it over, soaking the fish head, webbing and wood in soda. He figured it would wash off right away, but just as the pot hit the water, he thought he saw a little golden claw reaching for it. He told himself he was crazy as it dipped into the deep, but when he came back three days later and pulled the trap up, there was Monty."

"The aurum *Homarus Americanus,*" Owen says. He stops his scribbling for just a moment and looks up at me.

"Sure," I say, "the golden lobster. He looked dead as can be. Now, when we have a dead lobster in the tank at the shop, we call it a Monty. That's because Mrs. Barkley doesn't think any lobster should have to be buried without a name, so when Pa pulled this dead golden up out of the sea, he was pretty sad that it was already a Monty. He pulled it out of the pot to take a better look at it. It's not every day you come across a golden lobster, dead or alive. He set it down, and just as he let go of it, the lobster flipped over and ran straight for Pa's Coke. The whole bottle tipped over in the *Mary Grace* and Monty went after it, scrubbing his head into it and looking like he all-out enjoyed it. Basically, the golden lobster had played dead just to get another taste of that soda pop. After that, he really seemed to like the *Mary Grace.* He didn't try going overboard and would always sit in the captain's hub with Pa. But sometimes he got underfoot, so eventually . . ."

My stomach flips, getting to this part of the story.

Owen's pencil stops again. "What happened?"

"Well, he came home. And since my bedroom is on the ground floor and in the shade, we thought we'd set up an outdoor saltwater tank for him there. And I took care of him up until the day he snuck into my backpack to come to school. He got spooked by Officer Gallson's stupid siren and he . . . he . . ."

Owen's eyes are wide as I get to this part of the story.

"He dropped his crusher claw. Out of fear. So now . . ."

"He's missing an arm and he's golden," Owen says. "Predators will be watching for him."

"Owen!" I shout, not liking the sound of that.

"It's okay." Owen flips over and lies on his stomach next to me. "We'll have to work fast." He holds the book out over the edge of the platform so I can see it.

> *Monty*
> *Stats:*
> *golden*
> *likes fish heads*
> *likes Coca-Cola*
> *is not afraid of traps*
> *can play dead*
> *missing his crusher claw*
> *likes the Mary Grace*

"I think we need to re-create the original catch," Owen says.

"How? Steal my pa's boat?"

"Well, no, that doesn't seem practical, but we know he was here recently, as evidenced by the missing fish head. We just need to re-create that story here, where we know he's been hiding out."

I look up at the big face of the moon.

"We'd need a trap. That same kind, if possible," Owen says, scanning the ocean.

"That's easy," I say, feeling hopeful. "Pa has a bunch of old traps around the back of the house."

"We'd need the fish head and the Coke, too," Owen says. "If that's what he likes, he'll be drawn in by it. We can set a can or bottle out near the trap."

"That's easy, too," I say. "We have that in a cooler at Chickory and Chips."

"Now all we need is a boat," Owen says.

He gets up and looks through the telescope, out toward the Barley Light House and Goff's Pier. And I look up at Pisces and put my hand on my necklace, thinking that we'd better make this work, and fast.

Please, please, please, I think.

"By the beard of da Vinci!" Owen says, swinging his arm out and nearly hitting me in the shoulder.

"What is it?" I say, jumping up. "Is it him?"

"No," Owen says. "Look."

He holds the telescope steady as I line my eye up to it. It takes me a minute to really understand what I'm seeing. The light of the lighthouse is only brightening it in blinks and swoops. I squint and wait for the light to swirl back to this side, and when it does, I see that I'm looking at the end of a boat. Not a huge boat, but a rowboat, maybe. Wooden. I take the telescope in my hand and move it from right to left. The boat's split in half as though lightning cut it down the middle. Or like a giant picked it up and broke it in half over his knee and then stuck it, ends up, in the weeds.

"It's an abandoned boat," I say, disappointed Monty isn't waving through the lens.

"I know it is." Owen's standing at the front of the platform. "But think about it, Indie. We could replicate the *Mary Grace*."

"That won't work," I say. "It's all busted up. Ruined. A piece of junk."

"No," he says, "I mean, in the tree."

"What?" I say, trying to see what he's getting at.

Owen spins his pencil between his fingers. "We need a boat. We know Monty's here. We can't steal a real boat and set it up here with traps. We'll need to be innovative. We'll have to make a tree boat!"

"A tree boat?" I say.

Owen drops to his knees, grabbing his book. "It'll be my best innovation yet. We'll re-create the *Mary Grace* right here!"

"Yeah," I say, getting his idea in my head. "The front of that rowboat will be the bow. We can hoist it out here." I point toward the side facing the ocean. "And the back will be the stern. We can hoist it on this end." I point toward the opposite end, out toward the road. "We'll rig a wheel and a captain's hub right here," I say, pointing to the middle.

Owen starts nodding. "Hold on now." He opens to a fresh page.

Innovation XXXIII: Tree Boat

"We'll need to figure out how to hoist it and how many braces we're going to need to hold it," Owen says, looking up at me. "But you're good at that, from working in the scene shop."

I drop my hands. There goes that idea. I lean against the closest tree.

"I'm just there to help. I don't really know anything about building," I say.

Owen taps his eraser on his bottom lip.

"I know who'll know," Owen says. He tucks the pencil behind his ear and flips to a page. He turns it to me.

Sloth
Stats:
female
approximately 19 years of age
punk
vegan
good at building

"Sloth," he says.

"Sloth," I say.

He's right. She can help, if I can get her on my side for once.

Chapter 17

I'M JUST PUSHING the shampoo out of my hair when Bebe comes into the bathroom.

"Hey, just me," Bebe says.

"Yeah," I say. I'm used to her always barging in on me. I look through the side of the curtain as she hits the fan and starts to brush her hair one section at a time. Thirteen counts on the right, on the middle, and on the left.

"I set out your clothes on your bed, *and* a new bag," she says.

"Okay," I say as I grab the bar of soap and scrub my face.

"One, two, three," Bebe says, counting her brush strokes. I rinse my face, turn the water off and squeeze the last of it out of my hair. I reach around the curtain and my hand lands on a towel on the rack. I pull it into the shower.

"Raindrops on roses and whiskers on kittens," Bebe sings as I dry off and wrap the towel around me. I step out of the shower and go to my room, where I look at the clothes. Sloth is definitely not going to help me if I wear this into the shop. A pale blue shirt with flowers around one shoulder, jeans and a pair of fancy shoes with a buckle around the heel. A matching blue satchel, bedazzled with CHICKORY across the flap, sits sideways on the shirt.

"I can help you with your hair!" Bebe says from the other room. I hear her brush her teeth and spit.

I pick up the satchel and hold it in my hands, looking over every glittery letter. I flip it over and check the doorway to make sure that Bebe isn't looking.

"Indie, you almost ready? Your hair!" Bebe calls.

"Yeah, I'll be right in. Just let me change!"

I jump into the jeans and the blue flowery shirt, then I grab my Carhartts and roll them as small as they will go. I grab a plaid button-up, too, and toss that into the bag. I open my top drawer and pull out a pair of socks. Last, I reach out the window and pull the tool belt and sneakers out of my burlap bag. The sneakers are covered in sand. I hit them quickly against the siding of the house. The sand rains down into the grass. Then I tuck them into the satchel. I swing it over my shoulder so it's lying just over my hip. I go back into the bathroom and Bebe is just twisting a band around the end of one of her braids.

"That looks so much better!" Bebe says, noticing my bag before anything else.

"Thanks," I say, hoping that Sloth is not going to murder me for it. One thing I am sure of is that nothing in the shop is bedazzled. Nothing at all.

Bebe grabs the brush, faces me toward the mirror and

pushes the brush through my hair. Mom yawns and does a double take as she walks past the bathroom.

"Awww, wish I had my camera," she says, winking and going into the kitchen.

I roll my eyes.

Bebe stops. "What? You look cute. Just accept it."

For the first time in months and months Bebe is being nice to me. I hold my tongue and let her yank and pull.

When we head down Main Street, people wave. And not just to Bebe—they're waving to me, too.

"Chickorys!" Mr. Squiggles says as we head by. He gives a salute. "Top of the morning to you!"

Bebe smiles and nods and I do the same. We walk past Sandy's and Mrs. Callypso is standing outside with a tray of saltwater taffy.

"Would you like one, ladies?" she says, dipping the tray to meet us. I look over the little chunks of pink and white and yellow and green and finally spot my favorite, blue raz. I grab it up and pop it in my mouth. I let the sweetness melt on my tongue. Bebe takes one, too.

"Thanks, Mrs. Callypso," Bebe says.

"Thank you!" I say, and as we turn, there is a small cluster of tourists.

"Oh, can we get a picture of you two in front of the taffy window?" the lady asks, her lip gloss shining in the early-morning sun. Tourists always like quaint pictures with quaint locals—at least that's what Pa tells us.

"Sure," Bebe says, running her hand along her hairline, making sure nothing is out of place. She pulls me in next to her.

"Smile!" The lady with the gloss points her camera at us.

We do. Bebe sets a big old smile that's mostly teeth and I do the same.

"Adorable!" the lady says, and we head down the road toward Oceanside. Kelsey comes running up alongside Bebe.

"Did you just get your photo taken?" she asks.

"Yeah," Bebe says. "Just a snapshot."

"I bet it looked great." Kelsey grabs Bebe's hand and we turn onto the path and make our way to the front door of the theater. As we step up onto the porch, a blue Volvo zips past us and pulls into the parking lot. I look up and see Owen's face peering out the side window. He waves, and I go to wave back, but Kelsey's voice startles me.

"You don't know that freak, do you?"

I look from Owen to the ground to Bebe to Kelsey. Bebe's face all of a sudden looks pinched.

"Huh?"

"Do you know that freak with the glasses?" Kelsey asks. "Everyone is always talking about him. He's a huge nerd."

This sounds bad. "No, I don't know him," I say. The words roll out of my mouth before I really notice it. Just off my tongue and into the world, false and bold.

"Good," Bebe and Kelsey say together. I keep my eyes on my feet as we make our way around the side of the building.

"I'll see you later!" Bebe says.

"Sure." I head down into the stairwell.

Just opposite of Mr. Bluesey's office, I duck into the ladies' room. I undo the top of the bag and change quickly. I leave the braids in, but I put on my sneakers and my plaid button-up and my Carhartts. I look in the mirror and pop the earrings out of my ears. I take a deep breath. Now, to get Sloth on my side. To get Monty from the waves. Here goes nothing.

Chapter 18

BEFORE I EVEN get to the door, I hear Sloth's music slamming out into the hallway. *Not without a purpose and it's not without a fight. I've got three tales to tell you, so please sit tight.*

I push the door open and Sloth swings by, dancing like she's in the middle of a crowd. I jump back and lean into the door frame. I feel the thump of the bass through the wood—*boomboomboom*—and it seems to match the beating of my heart. As she swings back around, she comes up to me, jumping to the beat and singing in my face, "Not without a purpose, not without a fight."

She nods and sings and stares, the rings in her face bouncing.

"Hey, Sloth," I say, trying to figure out if this is the best way to start. But she keeps singing and she lifts up her right leg and stomps it to the beat, her whole body getting lower as she goes into an air guitar pose. How am I going to get her to notice me? That's when I remember what Bebe said, about following her lead. Maybe if I follow Sloth's lead, mimic her, she'll start liking me, start listening?

She jumps up and pretends to smash the guitar into the ground and then gets into headbanging around the room again. The *bompbompbomp* of the music in the door frame makes my feet start to jump a little. Just like that. Just a little teensy jump at a time. I drop my satchel in the doorway and nod to the beat, too, then flip my head around just like Sloth is doing. She spins past me, and I jump in right behind her, really feeling the music now, and to be honest, it feels kind of good, reeling around the room out of control. Sloth screams and whoops and I do the same. We dance like demons, and as the music comes to a stop, my body hardly knows which way is up. I stand still and the room takes a turn spinning and dancing as I teeter and try to get my eyes to focus.

"Yeah, Chickory. Feel it!" Sloth yells. I lose my balance and she grabs on to my shoulders with both hands.

I nod as her face doubles and bounces back and forth.

"Street Dogs," she says. "Best way to wake up."

"Nice," I say, catching my breath, but then Sloth lets go of me and I fall down in the middle of the floor. I watch as Sloth floats down next to me, and I sit for a minute until the room pulls back into one place. One standing-still place.

"That's as good as a power breakfast, which, if I may

say so, you look like you could use." I see her searching my face and put my hand up to feel around my eyes.

"Tired?" she asks.

"Stayed up reading," I say, dropping my hand into my lap.

She squints at me. "You look different today, Chickory."

"Yeah," I say.

"I dig it. You're prepared. You're in it." She makes a fist when she says *in it*.

She leans over, grabs her bag from the floor, opens it and pulls out a burrito. Then she gets up, takes a huge bite and waves me over to a detailed drawing that's laid out on the table. I follow behind. This is good. It's working. She's talking to me.

"Today, Plumtown Sheds Plus is going to deliver a gazebo." She points to a gazebo drawn on the thin vellum. "We need to alter it so it can roll on- and offstage. That means casters," she says.

I examine the drawing. I look toward the bottom of the plan and see the caster notes penciled in Mr. Bluesey's neat lettering. All capitals and all on a slant, like they're leaning backward.

"One set of fixed. One set of swivels," I read.

"Exactly," Sloth says through a mouthful of burrito. Then she pulls her wrench out of her pocket, swings it up over her shoulder and starts scratching between her shoulder blades again. "In the meantime, we also need to start putting together arches for the convent."

"Can I help?" I say.

Sloth stops chewing and looks at me. "Of course you can help."

"You can show me how?" I say.

"Of course I can," she says, tearing off another huge bite. "You grab the luaun." She points to some flat boards behind me. "And I'll grab the cut list."

As I walk over to the luaun, I see Owen's head poke into the doorway. I go over real quick.

"Did you ask her?" he says.

"Not yet. I'm working on it."

He steps back and looks at me from head to toe.

"You look different from this morning," he says. "Did you change?"

"Huh?" I say, trying to hide the fact that I know what he's talking about.

"I saw you this morning when we pulled in," he says. "I don't think you saw me, but I thought you were wearing something totally different."

"Oh yeah." I put my hands in my pockets. "I always change for the shop. Anyway, I gotta go. I'm getting close."

Owen smiles and disappears down the hallway, back into the props room.

"Indie?" Sloth turns, and she must spot Owen going down the hallway, because she says, "That kid's a piece of work, no?" I try reading her face to see if she's saying he's a piece of work like Bebe and Kelsey think he is or the opposite. But I can't really read her. She lifts an eyebrow at me and examines the cut list. I go over and grab the thin piece of luaun on the top of the pile, then return to Sloth in the middle of the floor and drop it flat onto the ground. As it lands, sawdust skitters up in a cloud around it.

We both look at the boards and Sloth pulls out her tape measure and runs it along one of them.

"Hey, uh, Sloth?"

"Hey, yeah?" she says as she pulls out a pencil and makes a little mark.

"Um, if I wanted to put an end of a boat in a tree, like as part of a tree fort, what kind of bracing would I need for that?"

She looks up at me, and her eyebrow lifts like there's a piece of string attached to the hoop ring and it's pulling it up.

"Just for a project," I say, "with my pa. We're, uh, we're working on a tree house and he has extra supplies from down at the dock and it's really unique and—"

"Huh," she says.

She goes over to the drafting table in the corner and pulls out a small piece of vellum. "Show me the plan."

I draw the four trees and the platform suspended between them, then I draw a boat end coming off one side of the platform, and then the flat rowboat end on the other side. It looks like a kindergartner drew it.

"Maybe I'll try aga—" I start to crumple the piece, but Sloth takes it out of my hand.

"Weight-bearing or non-weight-bearing?" she says.

"Uh, weight-bearing," I say, picturing the front piece jutting out over the rock outcropping and ocean. "Definitely weight-bearing."

"All right," she says, "and how big?"

I hold my arms out as far as they can go. "Each side is half of a rowboat, basically," I say.

"And how wide is your platform?"

I sit down and picture myself looking out across the platform into the ocean. I put my arms out to each side and Sloth opens her tape measure again, stretching it from the fingers on my right hand to the fingers on my left hand.

She jots down a few notes on the vellum. She draws one boat end with boards coming off of it like it has sprouted wings. She makes an arrow and writes *brace* at the end of it.

"Salvaged boat ends, right?" she says.

"Yeah," I say.

"To be safe, I would give it five braces. Use screws, not nails"—she points the pencil at me—"they hold better. Also, wouldn't hurt to tie the end off in one of the higher branches."

She draws a few lines straight up into the trees. She folds the vellum and hands it to me. "Here."

"Okay," I say. "Great, thanks."

I slide the vellum into my pocket, looking toward the door to see if Owen is there, not believing it was that easy. Not believing it's doable.

"You ready to work now?" Sloth says.

"Ready," I say. "Sorry, yeah, ready."

Sloth claps her hand down on my shoulder. It's much heavier than it looks. She squeezes. "You're okay, Chickory." She walks by her iPod and turns the music up, up, up until it fills the air around us. We get started.

Chapter 19

"BE BACK IN AN HOUR! Lunch break!" Sloth says as she hits a button on the wall that says LOADING DOCK DOOR underneath it. A half of the wall opens up, just like a garage door, letting sun stream inside. She walks out with her hands in her pockets and heads toward Main Street. I hear a shuffle behind me and Owen comes in.

"Did you get anything out of her?" Owen says.

I pull the vellum drawing from my pocket and unfold it, holding it up against the wall.

"She says we need screws, braces." I point to the five braces drawn on each side. "And a rope to make sure it holds. It can be secured onto a high branch."

Owen takes the paper and holds it up close to his face.

"I have ropes," he says.

"We can salvage the wood for the braces from the junk wood at the fort," I say. "I can grab some screws and a screw gun before I leave."

"We just need to figure out how to get the boat ends there," Owen says, folding the paper back up and handing it to me.

I hadn't thought of that. The boat ends are down at Goff's Pier. There's no way we can carry them back to Crawdad Beach. I chew my lip and watch as kids flood out onto the front lawn. I see Bebe and Kelsey and duck inside the doorway before they can spot me.

"Do you want to go and get lunch at Templeton's or Chickory and Chips? Aunt Peg gave me some money and I always think better on a full stomach," Owen says.

My stomach pangs away thinking about Mrs. Barkley's delicious clam chowder, but if Bebe spots me in my Carhartts and plaid and hanging around with Owen, she'll think I've turned back into what she hates the most.

"I'm not really that hungry, Owen," I say. My stomach growls.

"Did you know that a stomach growl is indicative of hunger? Your stomach muscles are contracting and forcing your digestive fluids and air around inside, making that gurgling noise."

"Ew," I say, not feeling much like eating anymore now that he's mentioned it.

"It's a fact, nothing to be ashamed of. Do you like the clam chowder at Chickory and Chips?" he says like he's some sort of mind reader. Stay strong, I think.

"Of course I do," I say, going over to the screw bin and grabbing a handful of the screws. "It's my mom's recipe, after all."

Owen walks over and takes a handful, too.

"That doesn't really mean anything," he says. "My mom makes lots of meals that I don't like."

I laugh as we put the screws into the bedazzled satchel. I try and keep them ends up so that they won't rip the fabric. A breeze comes through the shop door, lifting some of the sawdust off the floor and spinning it in little tornadoes. I grab the broom from the corner, tackle the tornado and start sweeping.

"There he is!" Aunt Peg's voice floats through the inner doorway and both Owen and I look up. She walks in, and right behind her comes a man and a woman. The lady is just like the lady out on the sidewalk this morning. Lip gloss and high heels. Not practical for the beach, but feeling fancy, I am sure. I can't help but suck my cheeks in and make a half trout pout.

"Oh, never mind about the chowder," he says real quiet, putting his hands in his pockets.

"There's my son!" the lady says, opening her arms. "We were hoping we could bring our boy out to lunch."

The man standing behind Mrs. Stone has his hair slicked over to one side, and he looks like he belongs in the movies. He jingles change in his pocket and chews his gum. I watch as Owen pulls his glasses off his face and wipes the lenses, then takes a deep breath and puts them back on. Something's not quite right. I can see that for sure.

"I'll see you later, Indie," he says quietly as he goes into his mother's arms.

"See you later," I say as I watch them walk back into the hallway.

Well, at least that frees me up for lunch, I guess. I finish sweeping, and by twelve thirty I am changed back into my Bebe outfit and running up the street for some delicious clam chowder.

Chapter 20

WHEN I GET UP to the tree fort later that night, Owen is already there. I can see the flashlight beam before I reach the outcropping. I push past the pine bough and scan the scene. He's got ten boards laid out and two long ropes coiled neatly on the ground. He's writing *brace* across the wooden boards with a huge marker.

I go over to the string hanging down from above. When I pull it, half of a fish head comes out of the water.

"He's been here," Owen says without looking up. "When I arrived, something skittered into the waves. I saw a golden tail dive out of sight."

"No way," I say, my heart nearly hitting the top of my head. "You saw him?"

"I think it was him." Owen finishes scribbling on the last piece of wood and caps the marker.

I look into the dark of the ocean, then up at the stars. "Please, please, promise me," I whisper.

"I told you that isn't going to work," Owen says, looking up through his glasses.

I shrug and go over to the boards, hanging the satchel filled with tools on a low branch.

"Looks like everything's all set. How long have you been here?"

"Approximately three hours," he says. "I came right after dinner."

I pull a handful of screws out of my pocket and drop them on the ground. "How?" I ask. "Everyone would notice if I left that early."

"My parents won't notice," Owen says, pulling his handkerchief out of his pocket and blowing into it. "They were into it. When they're into it, they never notice me. Man, my allergies are so bad tonight."

I guess by his changing the subject he doesn't really want to talk about it, so I sit down, testing the strength of one of the wood pieces and checking for warping like I've seen Sloth do. I close one eye, hold the board out in front of me, and peer down to the end.

Owen pulls out his Book of Logic and Reason.

"So I've been thinking a lot about how to get the boat ends here," he says, flipping to a page in the middle. He lays the book out on a rock and pushes it forward until the moonlight is splashing over it. When I look at the drawing, it appears to be a picture of a wagon. The boat ends are in it and they're tied down by rope.

"A wagon?" I ask. "They're still going to be super heavy. There's no way. I have an old Radio Flyer wagon, the kind with the handle, but I can guarantee that it isn't going to fit the boat ends in it."

"Right," Owen says, flipping the page, "which is why we can't use a traditional wagon. We need something big, with wheels and a hitch."

"A hitch?" I say.

Owen nods, the moon reflecting off his glasses as he moves his head up and down. I think on it for a second. There's Pa's truck, but that's not going to be a possibility. Maybe a bike and a sled. Then, just like that, a light in my head pops on. A golf cart.

"I might know where to find one of those," I say.

Owen's face breaks into a grin as he hands me the pencil. I take it and make a few adjustments to the drawing.

Twenty minutes later, my heart is nearly busting out of my chest as we make our way through the moonlight toward Mr. Crisco's property.

"I'm pretty sure this is illegal," I say.

"We're just borrowing it," Owen says. "If we were stealing, it would be illegal, and I would be morally opposed."

We hunker down and try to blend with the shadows as we near the shed.

"I don't like this," I whisper, checking the roadway for Officer Gallson.

"Do you want to move the boat or not?" Owen asks me.

"Of course I want to move the boat. How else are we

going to build the *Mary Grace*? How else are we going to get Monty?"

Owen nods sharply.

Besides, I tell myself, if it were the middle of the day, I could probably ask Mr. Crisco and he would tell me it's okay to go ahead and borrow it. Mr. Crisco is the nicest guy. He let me and Bebe use his golf cart before, when we had to send a shipment of fish from Chickory and Chips down to the yacht club on the other side of town and there was no one else to do it.

Owen and I get up to the shed and both spin and flatten ourselves against it like we're pinning our shoulder blades onto the outer wall. My mouth feels dust dry despite the humidity. I take a deep breath and sip my water bottle.

"Fluke, flounder, guppy, hake," I whisper, trying to calm the nerves in my stomach.

"What are you doing?" Owen asks.

I stop and look at him. "Oh, just saying fish names. It's a habit."

"Okay." Owen shrugs like saying fish names is the most normal thing in the world once explained. He looks around the corner of the shed.

"Locked?" I say, kind of hoping it is, 'cause I've been feeling like I have a bunch of guppies swimming around in my stomach every time I think about it.

"Nope. Plumtown has an extremely low crime rate. I looked it up. There's no reason to lock anything."

Until now, I think.

We slide the shed door open so that we both barely fit through.

The door sighs closed behind us and I look around. The light of the moon is filtering in from above. Kind of looks like we're in a cell, bars of light seeping in through the spaces between the boards, pretty much what it's going to look like for the rest of our lives if we get caught. I lick my lips and wipe the sweat streaming off my forehead. There are flowerpots and buckets, a set of old golf clubs leaned over next to a toolbox. Lots of rags with smudges all over them—hard to tell in the dark if it's blood or something else. Knowing Mr. Crisco, I'd imagine it's grease. There's also shears and trowels, rakes and shovels, all hanging from a rack on the wall.

And in the middle, there's exactly what we're looking for. Mr. Crisco's golf cart, with a trailer for hauling things. Mr. Crisco works for the golf course. He usually goes around collecting all the stray balls that people are too lazy to go and get themselves. And of course, the trailer is the perfect piece of equipment for hauling boat ends.

"Okay, now comes the tricky part," Owen whispers.

And he doesn't have to say anything about what the tricky part is, because I already know what he means: Now we have to get it out of here without anyone noticing.

"What's the plan?" I ask. "Get on, start it up and bust on out the door?"

"I was thinking something a little more discreet." Owen's examining the ignition.

"Okay, like what?"

"Well, first we need to make sure it's all clear."

I go over to a knot in the wall and peer out. I can see the Criscos' house from here. It's dead silent and dark as can be.

"Clear," I say.

Once I've checked for dangers, I go on over to the wall, looking for the key. I know exactly where it is from when we borrowed it last time.

My hand finds the brush broom and I reach under it, feeling for the hook. Sure enough, there it is. "You ready?" I say as I pull the key out and hand it to Owen.

He puts the key in the ignition but doesn't turn it all the way.

"Still clear?" he asks.

I go back over to the knot in the wall. I look out into the dark yard. The house is still quiet and not a single light is on.

I give Owen a thumbs-up but make sure to plant it in a ray of moonlight so he can see it.

Owen moves the shift. He's putting it into neutral so that we can push it out of here without starting the engine. He motions toward the shed door and I go over and lean my back up against it.

"Once you open it, if you can, come back and help me push," Owen says.

I take a deep breath and push the door open. The moon floods in like a spotlight. The door creaks on its hinges. In the quiet of the night it actually sounds like a dinosaur roaring. My heart flips like a fish out of water. I look at Owen, Owen looks at me. We both look toward the house. A light comes on.

Chapter 21

"GET BACK," I WHISPER. And we bolt back into the shed like there's a T. rex on our heels. The door makes as much noise shutting as it did opening. Once we're in the dark of the shed, I go over to the knot in the wall. Owen collapses next to me, breathing fast.

"We're done for," he says.

I shake my head, not wanting to believe it. I bite my lip as I peer out. 'Cause no golf cart means no boat ends, which means no *Mary Grace,* and that all means no Monty Cola. I slow my breathing down so it's barely audible. I see someone rustling around in the middle window on the second floor. It's Mr. Crisco. He's reaching for his glasses and trying to balance as he gets out of bed. Thank God for old slowness.

"What's the situation?" Owen says, looking through the cans on the ground next to him. I try to remain calm, but when I peer out again, it's the worst thing ever.

"Mr. Crisco's up and he's looking straight out his window into the lawn. Basically right at us," I whisper.

I watch as Mr. Crisco reaches for the bottom of the

window and slides it open. I curl back up and lean against the boards. I take two deep breaths. "Ballyhoo, bay anchovy, bigeye scad," I whisper.

"Nope, nothing out there, honey." Mr. Crisco's voice rings out through the night.

"You sure? I swear I heard something," I hear Mrs. Crisco saying.

"Not as far as the eye can see, darling," Mr. Crisco tells her. Then I hear the squeak as the window begins to shut.

"Oh, leave it open, Henry. It's so hot in here. Besides, I like to hear the ocean," she says.

"Yes, dear," Mr. Crisco answers.

"He's heading back," I whisper, putting my eyes back up to the knot in the wall, watching Mr. Crisco walk over to the bed and flip the bedside lamp out. The light in the shed goes back to the stale blue of the moon.

"It's all clear," I say, "but now the window's wide open. They'll definitely hear us. How are we going to get out of here?"

Owen's silent for a while. "Well, do you know anything about Mr. Crisco's sleep patterns?" he says finally.

"Sleep patterns?" I ask. "Like how much he sleeps?"

"Sure, that, and how quickly he falls asleep." Owen shakes one of the cans, then scowls and puts it down.

"Owen, I don't even know how quickly my mom falls asleep," I whisper. "How could I possibly know that?"

Owen shrugs and leans into the closest beam of

moonlight, examining a spray bottle in his right hand and another in his left.

"Never mind," I say. "We're going to have to wait a minute, no matter how you cut it."

I turn and lean my back up against the wall.

"We're in luck," Owen says, gripping one can and putting the other down.

"What?" I ask, 'cause nothing about this feels lucky at all.

"I found some WD-40," he says. He faces the can toward me.

"Okay," I whisper, reading the big block letters on the label. "What's that?"

"I used to use it on my vintage train set all the time. It's grease. We can spray it on the hinges and when we open the door again, it'll be silent as can be. It's basically stealth in a can."

WD-40. Good thing Owen has a vintage train set, I think. If only my fish knowledge panned out to something useful like that.

"All right, let's just hope he falls back to sleep quickly," I say.

"Well, it takes the average person seven minutes." Owen looks at his watch. "But you just never know with old people. Could go either way."

We sit in the quiet shed, barely breathing. I count to 60 seven times. Owen goes around the golf cart and sprays up a couple of the wheels, then goes over to the door and does the same with the hinges. He puts the can down and comes and sits next to me.

"So what comes after bigeye scad?" he says.

"Black margate, bluefish, blue marlin, bocaccio, bonefish, butterfish," I say, listing them down all the way to green sturgeon. Then I hear the teensiest little rumble coming from outside. I put my ear up to the hole in the wall, and I swear the little rumble is Mr. Crisco snoring in the night.

"I think we're good," I whisper. Owen gets up and he looks like a zebra with moving stripes as he passes through the moonbeams to the wheel of the golf cart. I go over and position myself against the shed door again.

This time, I push against it very lightly. Barely moving just in case it screams. But it swings easily. With the teensiest push it's halfway there. I open it the rest of the way and then go to the opposite side of the cart, grabbing ahold of one side, and we walk one slow step at a time into the night.

We make our way silently up Main Street, pushing that golf cart, and I am hoping beyond hope that no one decides to drive around at this hour, because this is going to be very hard to explain.

Chapter 22

WE'RE MUDDIER THAN A SWAMP monster when we get back to the golf cart with the second half of the rowboat. Both ends might as well have been planted deep in the mud like the rest of the weeds, the way they were stuck. I scrape the mud and sand off my arms as Owen ties the ends onto the trailer.

"You ready?" Owen is making a final knot.

"Yeah," I say, getting excited to see it all come together. To see if Monty will spot it from the waves. To see if we can really re-create the way Pa caught him.

"I'll hold it if you drive," Owen says, so I get into the front seat and take a look at the wheel. I look down at the pedals, at the key in the ignition. Last time we took this out, Bebe drove; I held the fish in a Styrofoam container. Still, it all seems easy enough. I've seen Mom and Pa drive a bunch of times. I've even seen Marty Shanks, the mulleted salami sandwich eater, drive a lawn mower, and if he can drive, that means that I can probably drive great.

I'm probably the world's best driver and I just don't know it yet. I start the ignition, grab ahold of the gearshift and push it to the spot marked *D*. I take a deep breath. I line the front of the cart up with the yellow line in the middle of the road and that's all I focus on until we're all the way back toward Chickory and Chips.

Now the only thing we have to do is get back, drop off the boat ends in the woods and put Mr. Crisco's golf cart back in his shed.

As we round the final corner on Main Street heading for Crawdad Beach, my heart skips a beat. The night begins to lighten. It can't be sunrise already, I think. I press my foot down heavy on the gas, and as we round the bend, I realize it's not the sunrise—it's something much, much worse. There's a car coming over the hill. Headlights cutting the night. I press the gas harder, but it doesn't jam down any more. It's going full throttle. We're almost to Crawdad Beach and if we can just pull in there and hide, we'll be all right. If we can make it there before the car crests the hill. I watch the car's headlights fly across the sand. It's coming closer and closer.

"Hang on!" I shout as I jam the wheel to the right and we just make it onto the far side of Crawdad Beach. The entry is bumpy and I can feel Owen grabbing on to the back of the seat with all his might.

"What's happening?" he says in my ear.

"A car's coming!" I shout, and as I say it, the car breaches the hill and I can see the headlights firing up the beach like it's daylight.

"Hurry, hurry, hurry!" I shout as the sand starts to bog down the wheels.

"We gotta bail," Owen says. "The sand's slowing us down!"

I hit the brakes and jump out. Owen jumps over the side of the trailer and starts untying the ropes, but the car is coming in too fast.

"Get down!" I say, curling up against the trailer. Owen lands next to me and the shadows get huge as the car comes closer. Please don't be Officer Gallson, I think, please don't be Officer Gallson. The engine and music are pumping out of the open window as it careens in. Owen and I are shoulder to shoulder, pressing as flat as we can into the wood.

"We're dead," I whisper.

But just as quickly as it comes, it passes on by. The music fades into the night and the lights disappear back to shadow. Owen puts two fingers up against his neck.

"My heart rate is way up!" he says, looking down at his watch. "My guess is that I'm exceeding my active heart rate by at least ten bpm."

I look at him and he looks at me. He's got sand in his hair and his glasses are sideways across his face and one of his sleeves is up while the other is down where it ought to be. We're a huge shaking mess. We're covered in mud and sand and hiding tucked up against a trailer in the middle of the night. Owen starts laughing first and then I lose it, 'cause it's just too ridiculous.

Once we compose ourselves, it only takes us a few minutes to undo the ropes. I pull one half of the rowboat off and Owen pulls the other. We make our way across the beach with the boat ends above our heads, like two crabs skittering in the sand.

We duck into the trees and have to slow down and navigate with care. When we push past the pine bough, we both drop our boat ends onto the ground and fall down.

"Water! Hydration," Owen says, and we sit up against tree trunks and suck down some water.

"If you rig the pulleys . . . I can put braces on these . . . ," I say between gulps. "And we can screw them in when we hoist them up."

"I like your thinking," Owen says, water gushing down his chin.

So we build it. Owen hooks up the pulleys, then pulls the boat ends up, and I screw the braces into the trees just the way it is in Sloth's drawing. We scan the trees out toward Crawdad Beach every once in a while with the telescope in case the screw gun is waking up the neighborhood, but it's all quiet. Before long we have the front and the back of a boat secured. Owen and I both sit on the platform and stare out at the open sea.

"C'mon. C'mon, Monty!" I say. Owen pulls out a can of white paint and we pop the cap off with the end of a screwdriver. I take a paintbrush and dip the end in.

I lean over the bow from my spot on the inside and paint:

Mary Grace II

I cover a yawn as I pull the paintbrush back in, resting the brush on the lid. My eyes feel like drooping down right here and now.

"That's nice," Owen says, leaning against one of the tree trunks. "We did it. Now we just need the Coca-Cola and the trap."

He yawns, too, and stretches his hands to the sky as if he's just waking up in the morning, and as soon as I see him do that, I can't help but do it again.

"We should pack it in for the night, I guess," I say.

As I lift the lid up and place it back onto the paint can, a distinct splash happens offshore. Both Owen and I run to the front of the boat, searching the waves, and sure enough, just below, a lobster tail flips and flaps across the surface of the water as if he's giving us a sign. I rush to the ladder and clamber down. Then I jump into the water.

"Monty," I shout, holding out my arms, but just as I do, Monty goes back under. I drop my hands.

I spooked him again.

"That's okay, Indie," Owen says from above. "We'll get him tomorrow night. We just need to rig the trap."

"Yeah, tomorrow," I say.

Owen comes down the ladder and we make our way back through the trees. When we hit Main Street, we go our separate ways. I head up Brookrun Drive, feeling tired but just right. It's been an all-around great day. Bebe and I are getting along. Sloth didn't get mad at me—she even helped me. And Owen and I got one step closer to catching The Lobster Monty Cola. Real close, I think. I feel pretty good as I climb in my window. I change into my nightshirt and slide into bed. I look up at the glowing stars on my ceiling. I almost think I hear Bebe singing somewhere off in the house. Must be in her sleep or maybe just in my ears. I shake my head. But it still comes my way, what Pa calls her lonely sailor voice. I rest my eyes and listen, the sound reminding me of another time.

"Can you help me?" she said, grabbing my hand. "I've got a big wish."

"Of course," I said.

We lay down on our backs on the front porch. Bebe's feet facing the door. My feet facing the yard. Our heads together in the middle. From there, we watched the stars come out. Our hands spun like antennas in the air as we traced and said hello to the constellations as they woke up in the sky.

"Hello, Aquarius," Bebe said.

"Hello, Aries," I said, pointing to the first star in the constellation, then dropping to the next and back again.

"Hello, Al Rischa," Bebe said, pointing at Pisces' brightest star.

"Hello, Pisces," I said. "Hello, fish."

Bebe traced from the nose of one of the fish down to its tail, and I did the same with the other side. From nose to tail and back again.

"Pisces, please promise me . . . ," she sang. I turned my head to see Bebe clasp her Pisces charm with her other hand. "Perfection." She sang it again. As one melodic sentence. "Pisces, please promise me perfection. Perfection."

"You're already perfect, Be," I said.

I thought about how neat and tidy she always was. How she had so many friends and a perfect smile. And how she had a voice straight from the sea. But as I watched her, she pinched her eyes closed and her eyelids quivered with the force of the wish. It was a real serious one. Like she never believed it, like she had a lot of growing to do. I looked back up at the stars and held on to my charm.

"Pisces, please promise me," I said, and Bebe sang the words behind my words. I stopped, thinking about what I could wish for. "Happiness."

"Perfection and happiness," Bebe whispered.

"Perfection. Happiness," I whispered.

We lay there for a long time, holding on to those wishes. Holding on to our charms. Tracing the stars.

The voice in the night disappears into voices in my dreams. And I fall fast asleep.

Chapter 23

"INDIE, INDIE." I groan and pry my eyes open. Bebe's face comes into focus right above me.

"I left your outfit right on your chair," she says, swallowing her last word with a yawn. "I told Kelsey I would meet her early at Crawdad Coffee House. Okay?"

I sit up in bed. Bebe rubs her eyes with the palms of her hands, then hums as she leaves the room.

I walk over to the desk and pick up the outfit. Jean shorts today, with an *Annie* T-shirt, complete with an outline of Annie and her dog, Sandy, smiling out of the front. I start switching into it. I can hear Mom rustling around in the kitchen. The teakettle goes off as I button up the shorts and pull on my shirt. The front door slams and my head snaps up. I rush to the bathroom, thinking that I'd better start looking a lot livelier than I am feeling. I go in and splash some water on my face, trying not to walk, look around or sound like a zombie. The cold water stings, waking up my eyes and making my skin feel tight all around. I wipe my cheeks and hands with a towel and head into the dining room.

"Morning, kiddo," Mom says, pushing a lid onto a Tupperware container.

"Bebe left?" I say, my brain trying to wrap around what she was talking about. About going to a meeting or something?

"Yeah, she said she had to meet Kelsey early to rehearse the dinner party scene. You want some breakfast?"

"Nah." I couldn't eat right now if I tried. My body and bones are so tired from running around all night, I feel like I'm a ship off course.

I go straight over to the door.

"Going barefoot?" Mom asks.

I stop and look down. My head is not attached to my shoulders. I slap my forehead and go straight back into my room. I grab the bedazzled Chickory satchel and throw in a pair of khaki shorts. Then I pull out my second drawer and grab the first T-shirt that I can get. I push on the flip-flops that I didn't even notice Bebe left neatly under my desk chair. I go to the window, open it all the way, reach down to the ground, grab my tool belt and sneakers and toss them in my satchel, too.

Then I head back out the door.

"That's better!" Mom says, handing me the Tupperware. I take it and a kiss on the cheek.

As I pass Crawdad Coffee House, I hear a loud knocking on glass, and when I look up I see Bebe and Kelsey waving at me. I wave back as they turn toward their hot chocolate. Bebe blows on the marshmallows. As I pass, I notice she looks tired. Tired like me. My reflection showing off my puffy eyes, and her face, staring out at me, showing off her puffy eyes, too.

But why is she so tired? She couldn't have been awake when I came in. I trip as I get toward the front of Oceanside Players and catch myself just before I hit the sidewalk. As I regain my footing, I take a quick peek over my shoulder. No one saw it. No one's around. But one thing's for sure: It's going to be a long day.

Chapter 24

SLOTH SLAMS THE BOARD down right next to my ear and I pop awake with a start, pulling my earlobe to try and get the ringing out.

"I'm up," I say, reaching for my hammer with the other hand.

"Nice try, Chickory," she says, sitting down on the bench across from me. She puts her arms around her knees. "What's going on?"

"Huh?" I say.

"What's going on?" she repeats, looking me up and down. "You look exhausted. You've got one earring in."

My hands shoot up to my ears. I find one earring dangling, the other ear empty. I pull the earring out real fast and stuff it into my pocket.

Sloth keeps talking. "You've got one sock on. You keep nodding off. What's your deal?"

I look down at myself and realize I didn't do a very thorough job of changing from my Bebe outfit to my shop outfit in the bathroom.

"I'm just reading a really good book," I say. "Can't get

to sleep. Up all night. I guess"—I look down at my sock—
"I guess it's just making me forgetful."

"Oh, really?" she says. "I like reading. What are you reading?"

"You probably wouldn't like it," I say.

"Try me," she says, running her tongue along her teeth.

I try and think of a title, but my brain feels like it's stuck in a mud pit. I stop talking altogether and stare at her nose ring.

Sloth leans in. "Chickory," she says quietly, resting her arms on the table between us. "Officer Gallson is down on Crawdad Beach checking out a stolen golf cart, covered in mud and sand."

This sentence makes my head pop back, because it's then I realize that we got so caught up in making our boat that we completely forgot to bring Mr. Crisco's cart back. And I was so tired walking down to the theater that I didn't even notice it. She ignores my look and keeps on talking.

"I'm not going to blame you or judge you, but I will say that you do seem to have a little bit of sand in your hair this morning. And your shoes are a mess. Caked in mud, actually. And what's this under your fingernails?" She grabs them and I pull them back. Seeing that each nail is ringed in dirt.

"And hey, I noticed that you had a few shop tools with you this morning. What could you be using those for in the evenings?"

I jerk my head over to my bag. The tool belt is spilling out the side. "Sorry, Sloth," I say. "I should have asked you first. It was for the, er, the tree fort." I scramble around, looking for a clear thought.

She rolls her eyes and crosses her arms. "Your pa doesn't have tools? None at all? I find that very hard to believe."

I swallow hard. "Sorry." I'm straight out of excuses, but lucky for me, she gets going.

She waves her hand in front of my face. "It's fine, kid. You can borrow stuff if you need it. But this"—she pulls my arm so my hands are out in front of her again—"all I'm saying about this is that you might want to get yourself down to the costume shop, find a hat and a new pair of shoes and go wash your hands."

I nod.

"And Owen, too!" she says. "His boots dragged huge mud cakes into the hallway and I had to vac them up, the chunks were so big. I'm just saying . . . so that people don't start suspecting anything and blaming you for things that happened while you were snug in your bed, *reading*. Got it?"

I nod again and get to my feet.

"Once you've got a hat and new shoes, please go to the cot in the green room and take a twenty-minute nap. I will tell you when it's over. I need you awake and alert to get this gazebo done. Safety—"

"Safety first in the shop, gotitthanks!" I say, rushing down the hall. I duck my head into props and I see Owen facedown on the desk.

"Owen," I whisper.

He lurches up. "I got it, Aunt P—" he says, still half asleep.

"It's Indie. You're needed in costumes, stat!" I say.

Owen picks up his book, rolls it up and puts it in his back pocket. He rubs his eyes as we head down the hall. "What's going on?" he says.

"We forgot the golf cart is what's going on!" I hiss.

I hear Owen draw in a breath, and when I look back, he's pushing his glasses up on his nose in a nervous sort of way. He looks all of a sudden like he is one hundred percent awake.

"The cops are down there now. Sloth sent me to change because I have mud and sand everywhere."

"Did you tell Sloth?"

"No, she just said I look suspicious. Also said to go and get you. Sh-she knows something's up."

Owen and I peer around the door of the costume shop. No Mrs. Clark, just a bunch of clothes for the taking.

"All right," I say, spotting us in the mirror. Owen's hiking boots are loaded with mud and sand, too, despite whatever chunks fell off in the hallway. The treads are huge and caked in it.

"New shoes," I say as we turn to face the shoe rack. I survey the selection, looking through loafers and buckled shoes.

"Maybe over here," Owen says, looking in a bin. "I think that rack is for this show." I go over and look in, too. There are piles and piles of shoes of every kind. And plenty of sneakers. Velcro, lace-up, and some that don't require laces at all. I dig around and find a pair of sneakers about my size and pull them up out of the bin. They're tied together as a pair. Pumas, similar to the ones I'm wearing now. I loosen the laces, throw my current pair in the trash and slide them on. Owen pulls out a pair of loafers and does the same.

"Now," I say, scanning the shop. There's a rack near the shoes that is filled with hats, but like Owen says, that's probably for the show. Against the back wall, there's an entire shelf with hats stacked upon hats. We both go over and survey the shelf. Bowlers, beanies, baseball. I scan from one end to the other and pick up a flat cap, something you might see a golfer wearing. I put my hair up on top of my head and press the cap on.

"Yes!" Owen says, pulling a hat out from under a big

furry winter cap. "It's a vintage aviator cap!" He pulls on the brown leather hat with goggles attached to the top. The earflaps swing down to his chin.

"The idea is to draw *less* attention to ourselves," I say.

Owen ignores me, admiring himself in the mirror on the opposite wall. Then he turns to the wall of jackets, pants, skirts and dresses. He starts examining a gray vest, but drops it after a second and looks toward the doorway. I step back into a rack of pants.

"Do you hear something?" Owen says.

I put my hand out to the rack of clothes to stop the hangers from swinging into each other and listen. It sounds like footsteps coming this way. I get down and peer out into the hallway between two von Trapp dresses. They're covered in big flowers, the ones for the curtain dress scene.

It's Kelsey and Bebe.

"Oh," Owen says, "I need to talk to them about their props for the thunderstorm scene."

He's about to step out and go to them.

"Nope, we're not supposed to be here. We better hide!" I say, pushing Owen back behind a rack of pants. I duck in, too, until we're both pressed against the wall behind wool tweeds and corduroys.

Owen holds his palms up at me and mouths, "Why?"

I just shake my head and press my lips together.

"All right, girls, time for measurements. Kelsey first, please."

That's Mrs. Clark.

Kelsey and Bebe chat about how they can't wait for their costumes for the dinner party scene, and how elegant it's going to be. And it's kind of dark and cozy back here. And warm. I yawn and after a while Owen spreads out along the whole rack and I do the same in the opposite direction till we're back to back, and it's pretty comfy. It takes them forever, and after a little while I hear Sloth call through the doorway, "Hey, have you seen Indie or Owen? Peg and I can't find them."

"Sorry, dear, haven't seen them," Mrs. Clark says.

"Ew," Kelsey says. "Do you think they're off together somewhere?"

"I highly doubt it," Bebe says.

I hear Owen shift behind me as he listens, but I can't see his expression.

"Right," I hear Sloth say as she walks away. And I get a feeling in my belly, like a balloon shrinking.

Chapter 25

AS I MAKE MY WAY UPSTAIRS, I pull the earrings from my pocket and put them back in my ears. Then I adjust the hat on my head. I consider tossing it back in the costume shop, but there's no way I can do that. We have to walk past Crawdad on the way home and I don't want bored old Gallson getting suspicious. I make sure I'm wearing the jeans and the *Annie* shirt that Bebe gave me this morning. I put the sneakers in my satchel and make sure that I'm wearing two flip-flops, not one. I tuck a few wisps of hair up into the cap and meet Bebe upstairs in front of the building. She's standing with Kelsey. She hurries over to me.

"What's with the hat?" She runs a hand through her hair and neatens her shirt so the seam is running straight along her shoulder rather than sitting crooked. "I leave you for one morning and you change the whole deal. What is with you today?"

But then something weird happens. Kelsey comes over and grabs my arm. Grabs my arm like we're best pals.

"Wow," she says, "I love that hat on you. I was looking at one just like it last weekend."

I stand up a little straighter as Bebe slaps on a toothy smile and comes around to my other side, linking my free arm. I must be getting pretty good if even Kelsey Duncan likes my choice of hats.

"Oh, thanks," I say as we fall into step.

"Where did you get it? We should totally get matching ones," Kelsey says.

"Count me in," Bebe says.

We turn the corner and head down Main Street.

"It was a gift, uh, from Gramma," I say. I catch Bebe giving me a glance out of the corner of my eye, but I just ignore it 'cause I'm on a roll.

"It's lovely," Kelsey says, flipping her braids. "If you find out where she got it, I might go and get one."

"Oh, we'll definitely check with her," Bebe says.

We walk up to The Manors and Kelsey breaks off. "Well, I had better run. I'll see you guys tomorrow." She waves and heads down the cul-de-sac.

Bebe and I keep walking arm in arm for a minute until we're out of sight of the pretty houses. Then she drops my arm.

"Gramma got you that hat?" she says.

"Not exactly," I say.

"Well, where did you get it, then?" she asks as we walk past Sandy's Saltwater Candies. I look in and instead of drooling over the taffy spinning in the window, another display catches my eye. The marzipan treasure chest with a skull sitting next to it.

"Sloth gave it to me," I say.

"Really?" she says. "Why would Sloth have anything like that? She always has her hair in spikes."

"Yeah, well, that's just it," I say, scanning the beach up ahead. "She can't use her hats much anymore, so she gave one to me."

I spot Officer Gallson walking back and forth along Main Street. He's on the other side of the road and coming our way. I lick my lips and start speeding us along.

"Did Mom want us to pick something up from Mrs. Barkley?" I ask.

"She didn't mention anything," Bebe says, kicking a small stone into the road.

"I think she did," I say. I step onto Chickory and Chips' front porch as quickly as possible. Officer Gallson is nearing his squad car, which sits out front. The bell rings as we duck past Barnacle Briggs and into the shop just in the nick of time.

"Well, hello, girls!" Mrs. Barkley says, spinning. Her seashell earrings clink together as she turns.

"Hey, Mrs. Barkley," Bebe and I say.

"What brings you two in today?"

Bebe goes past the cracker and preserves shelf, over to the basket of samples.

"Indie thought that Mom wanted us to pick something up for dinner," she says.

Mrs. Barkley cocks her head to one side. "Funny, I didn't get any messages about that."

"Maybe not," I say, following Bebe over to the samples. I pick up the little knife and dip it into a jar of apricot jam. I pull out a gob and spread it slowly onto a wafer. Then stuff it into my mouth.

"You girls just want snacks, don't you?" Mrs. Barkley asks, winking at me.

I smile and make another one while peeking out the shop window at the same time. I watch as Officer Gallson pulls his radio out of his squad car and starts talking into it.

Mrs. Barkley puts her elbows on the counter and rests her head on her hands.

"Quite a bit of excitement we've had today," she says, following my gaze.

"I bet," Bebe says, going over to the lobster tank. "Did they figure out who the criminals are yet?"

My mouth goes dry and the cracker crumbs seem to skitter down and stick in my throat. I drop the butter knife.

"Not yet. They don't seem to have any leads, either," Mrs. Barkley says.

I swallow the lump in my throat and go over next to Bebe to check for Montys. Dead Montys, not actual Monty. Bebe comes up next to me and we both scan the tank. "There might be a dead one there?" She points at the glass.

I just barely start to look for it, but I spot Officer Gallson through the watery tank. His head's distorted by the moving water and the tank glass, but it's definitely him and he's heading straight for the door. Without even realizing it, I grab Bebe's arm and dive behind the produce rack in the middle of the store.

"What are you—"

"Shh." I put my hand up to my lips. Bebe presses hers together and starts neatening her hair. But she doesn't get up. She doesn't go out there. She's being an ally.

"Pam, how are you, darling?" Officer Gallson says as he comes inside.

I know Mrs. Barkley doesn't like it when Officer Gallson goes and calls her "darling," but she's too nice to say anything against it, so she uses her usual manners.

"Fine, Johnny. How can I help you today?"

"I just popped in to let you know I'm headed out. But if you see anything, you give me a call, okay? I'll come right back over."

"Sure thing," Mrs. Barkley says. Bebe scoots to the edge of the produce stand and watches around the corner. A second later the bell rings again.

"He's gone, spaz," Bebe says, standing up and dusting herself off.

"What was that about?" Mrs. Barkley asks, tucking the phone number card under the corner of the cash register.

I stand up and dust myself off, too. "Oh, nothing," I say. "I guess we had better go."

"You're still mad at him about Monty, aren't you?" Bebe says.

I nod and look from Bebe to Mrs. Barkley.

"Sure thing," I say. And that is true. I *am* still mad at him about Monty. Just a couple of other things piled on top of it as well.

"I don't care for him much, either," Mrs. Barkley says, and gives me another wink. Bebe and I giggle.

We walk to the door, and just before we get outside, I spot the cooler and remember the Coca-Colas.

"Mrs. Barkley, can we take a Coke?" I say.

"Sure, dear," she says. I reach for the handle and pull out a Coke for each of us.

"I don't want a Coke," Bebe says. "Kelsey says they're not very good for you. The carbonation can hurt a singing voice."

I still take two out.

"Bye, Mrs. Barkley!" I say.

"Bye, now," Mrs. Barkley says as I carry the Cokes out the door.

"I said I don't want that," Bebe repeats as we head toward home.

"You might later," I say, but really, I'm not thinking of leaving it for Bebe at all. I'm bringing it to the *Mary Grace II* and we're going to get Monty back. Tonight.

Chapter 26

I PUT ONE BOTTLE of Coke in my right pocket, then I put the other bottle in my left pocket. That's why I love Carhartts. There's plenty of room for storage in them. I climb out my window and duck around the side of the house to the shed, where Pa keeps row upon row of his fishing supplies. I grab one of the buoys and its line and pile it on top of an old wooden trap. Last, I head over to the muck bucket and dig my hand into the mess. I grab out two fish heads and throw them into the trap as well. Then I lean down and swing the whole thing onto my back so I'm holding the trap with the buoy against my spine. It's a heck of a lot heavier than I thought it would be. I head out across the lawn, the whole mess weighing me down all the way to the road. Once I reach Main Street, I have to stop and take a few deep breaths. I hear a little rumbling to my right and see the street light up. My heart flip-flops. Even though I'm already tired, I grab that trap, throw it back over my shoulder and run as fast as I can until I reach the tree line. The whole beach is lighting up—the headlights are painting it white from one end to the other. I dive into the trees and roll out of sight. Then I hunker down low to look past the bough.

The car slows and right away I can see it's Officer Gallson. He rolls his window down. I hear music bounce out into the night and combine with the sound of the waves. I get down flat as he pulls his Maglite out, flips it on, and scans from one end of the beach to the other. Even though Mr. Crisco's golf cart is long gone, when he reaches where it had been marooned, his flashlight stays there for a minute. Holding steady on the spot.

He spins it back toward me and I duck my head way down so none of the light lands on my skin. I watch the beam pan over my head and onto the leaves in front of me. As the light catches them, their underbellies glow green before my eyes.

I hear him whistle as the light disappears, and he pans it over to the shop. It scans over Barnacle Briggs and then bounces back again, inspecting him top to bottom. I guess once Mr. Gallson sees it's just a wooden pirate, he moves along. He rolls his window up, and his rickety old squad car squeaks and moans its way down the street. I take a deep breath and wipe my forehead clear of sweat. I watch until his car is long, long gone. Till I can't even see one little dot of red taillight. Then it's safe to move. I grab on to the rope mesh of the trap and head into the woods.

"What took you so long?" Owen says as his head pops over the side of the tree boat. He's wearing the aviator cap and a headlamp over the top of that.

"Officer Gallson," I say. "He's on patrol!"

Owen kills his headlamp. "I was wondering if he would be out. It was all clear when I got here," he whispers, climbing down the ladder and jumping onto the milk crate.

"He's gone now," I tell him as I drag the lobster pot past the pine bough. "A little help here!"

Owen comes over and grabs one end and I grab another and we pull it to shore, right under the tip of the bow above us.

I untie the bait bag from the trap and put a few fish heads in the mesh pouch. Like I've seen Pa do a million times. Then I pull out a Coke bottle. Owen takes it and twists the cap off.

"All right, douse the bag," I say.

Owen pours the fizzy drink all over the bait bag and all around the wooden trap. The soda fizzles along the mesh rope. Owen turns the bottle bottoms up and sends the last over the top. Then he grabs a piece of string from the spool and brings it over.

"What's that for?" I say.

He ties a loop around the bottle, lowers it into the lobster pot and ties it onto the rope mesh.

"Nice idea," I say, thinking that even when the ocean

dilutes the soda, Monty'll see the Coke bottle. He'll come running. Owen's really getting into his head.

I pick up the trap and hand the buoy to Owen. "Can you secure the buoy to the end of the boat so it looks like it's hanging out just in front of the bow?" I say.

"You bet," he says, grabbing the buoy. He throws it over his shoulder and climbs back up the ladder. He swings the buoy over a branch so it's hanging out in plain sight and gives me an A-OK sign.

I grab the trap and jump down into the water. It's freezing at night and goose bumps creep across my arms and legs as I go in up to my knees and then to my stomach. I stop there and hold the trap out. Then I fling it as hard as I can. It flies and snaps at the end of the line and sinks into the waves. I muscle back toward the tree house and drag myself onto the rock. The warm air feels much colder now that I'm drenched in water.

I go over to the milk crate, climb on, reach for the ladder and climb up to the boat. Once I get there, I see Owen already has his night-vision magnification goggles on his head. I flick the drops off my legs and go over to the telescope.

"C'mon, Monty," I say, looking out past the buoy and into the waves. "I hope it works."

For a few minutes, we both just look out into Plumtown's coast. I watch for the line to jump, for any sign that something might be happening. But the buoy bounces gently with the waves of the ocean. I crawl into the bow of the boat and lean up against the side, watching the buoy sway.

"Hey, Indie?" Owen says, lifting his night-vision goggles up onto his aviator cap.

"Yeah?" I say, leaning my head on the rough wood and looking back toward him.

He steps into the bow, and the rope that is securing it in place creaks the teensiest little bit. "Remember earlier when we were hiding in the costume shop?"

"Yeah?" I say.

"I couldn't help but wonder why Bebe said that . . . about how you weren't hanging out with me."

My throat feels like it's filling in with sand. I was hoping he wouldn't notice, but a kid with a book about observation, well, I should have known. Still, what am I supposed to say? I know what it's like to be made fun of, and it hurts, and I don't see why I should have to make Owen feel like that for no reason.

I just shrug. "I don't know. That was really weird!"

"Oh," Owen says, then he smiles, sitting down next to me. "So you don't know what she was talking about?"

"Nope. I think she just doesn't know anything about working backstage, so she didn't understand that we would know each other."

Owen frowns a little. "Funny," he says. "Kelsey said 'ew.' And Bebe—I thought I sensed some sort of judgmental tone in her voice."

"She always sounds like that," I say. And that's not a lie. Besides, it's a lot better than saying, *Oh, I pretend not to know you because I'm trying to be a better Chickory and that includes being a good, non-embarrassing sister. You're a nerd and nerds are embarrassing.* Owen's weird, but saying something like that could hurt anyone's feelings.

"All right," Owen says. "Just making sure. I mean, I hate being a disappointment. You know?"

"Yeah, I know," I say, because I really do know. I know all about that. "She was just talking."

And as I say it, the buoy spins and bounces, wrapping itself around the branch one way and then the other. Both Owen and I jump up.

"Is it him?" I shout, grabbing ahold of the buoy and hauling it backward toward the platform. I can barely get it to move, like the waves have become a big fist, holding the trap close to its heart.

"Owen!" I shout as I start to slide forward.

"Whoa!" he shouts, grabbing on to the end, too. We both lean back and pull, hand over hand, until the sea lets go and the trap slides out of the water, dropping a shower below it.

"Look!" Owen shouts as the trap spins in the air below us. There's The Lobster Monty Cola, shining gold in the moonlight. The only thing is, he's not in the trap. He's clinging to the side of it, trying to get the bottle out through the mesh.

"Yes!" I shout.

Just then, Owen drops the rope.

As hard as I try to stand my ground, I lurch forward straight up against the bow. I jam to a halt as the wood presses into my stomach. The trap inches its way back to the water. It spins and gurgles as it goes under.

"Owen, what the—" I turn to glare at Owen but freeze. There's a light filtering through the trees, coming from Crawdad Beach.

"Did Officer Gallson have a Maglite?" Owen says, backing toward me.

"Yeah," I whisper. Dropping the rest of the rope in the bow.

"He must've heard us."

I look down to see if Monty is still clinging to the trap, but as far as I can see, Monty's not there anymore. My eyes fill with tears as the leaves rustle. Officer Gallson's coming in fast. We've got no choice but to move.

Chapter 27

"GO, GO, GO," Owen says as we both head over to the ladder. Owen goes down first, pulling his night-vision goggles over his eyes. I follow as we sneak into the dark of the trees. We head away from the beach, the opposite direction of Officer Gallson, and I think we're gaining some distance when Owen stops so fast that I run smack into him.

"What is it? You okay?" I ask.

"Yeah," he says so quietly that I can barely hear him. "It's just, I—I left my book."

"Just leave it," I tell him.

"I can't," he says. "I don't go anywhere without it. Besides, it's got my name all over it. It's incriminating evidence."

I hear Officer Gallson brushing through the trees. It's so dark, I can barely see Owen, but I can sense he's going to head back that way, and a second later, he presses something into my hands. I feel around it. It's his night-vision goggles.

"Owen?" I whisper, closing my fingers around them,

but he's already moving as quickly and quietly as he can back toward the boat. I take the goggles and pull them on, then I hunker down in the shadows, way down so my belly is on the ground. My shirt, which is still wet from bringing the trap into the water, presses against my skin and makes me shiver. I stare up at the tree boat. Officer Gallson's flashlight, now green through the lenses of the night-vision goggles, bounces toward him through the trees. I feel like I have scad flitting around in my stomach. I put my hand over my belly to try and tell my nerves to quiet down.

"Monkfish, ocean perch, peanut bunker," I whisper as I watch Owen reach the platform.

"Hurry, hurry, hurry," I breathe.

I see Owen's silhouette against the moonlit sky. He looks like a little green action figure against the huge fluorescent orb of the moon. He reaches down and picks up his book, rolls it and puts it in his back pocket.

As he turns toward the ladder, I see the pine bough shake and Officer Gallson's hand wraps around it to push past it. Next thing I know, the Maglite is lighting everything up, so I have to flip the night-vision lenses up onto my head. I squeeze my eyes closed and then blink several times, trying to get the spots out. I see Owen dive low. I lick my lips and tell myself to stay put. Gallson comes into the clearing, shining his flashlight this way and that. I press myself into the earth and keep my eyes on that tree boat. I see the aft move the teensiest bit. Owen must be hiding in that boat end. I watch the rope and the braces pull and stretch with the weight of him. Please don't let Gallson notice it. Please.

Officer Gallson is going back and forth over the *Mary Grace II* with his flashlight, as if he's painting the boat with the beam. He steps over to it, steps up onto the milk crate and yanks on the ladder. The branch bends as he tests his weight on it.

I sit up on my knees. He's actually going to go investigate. He's going to go up there. Owen'll be trapped. C'mon, think clear, I say in my head. Now Officer Gallson has both feet on the bottom rung and is bouncing it a tiny bit. The branch swings and creaks with his weight. I have to do something. I have to do something fast. Then it occurs to me—I'm not the fastest in the school, but the way that bough is bending, it's guaranteed I could outrun him.

That's when I do the craziest thing. I stand up in the middle of the woods and I do a half laugh, half war cry straight into the night sky. Something like I hear on Sloth's music all the time.

"Who's there?" Officer Gallson shouts, jumping off the ladder and pointing his flashlight out in my direction. I pull the night-vision goggles down over my eyes, turn and book it through the trees.

Officer Gallson's flashlight bounces around like crazy as he follows behind. He's jostling it so much, it hardly manages to touch me at all, but I see it, like a green ray bouncing from one side to the other. I lure him away from Owen, away from the *Mary Grace II*, away from Monty.

I jump over a downed log. I'm taking a serious lead. I can barely hear Office Gallson huffing and puffing, he's so far back.

I'm just starting to wonder where I am when car headlights and the rumble of an engine zip by in the road out in front of me. I can't go out into the moonlight. It's safer here in the shadows. I turn around, tread backward over to a tree and put my foot on the lowest branch. I see him closing in. A looming green monster. He's disoriented, though, sending his flashlight beam off to the right, like there's something over there. I climb as quietly as I can. And it's quieter than I knew I could go.

"Who's there?" Officer Gallson says to the trees over to my left. "Give up now and you won't get into trouble."

Yeah, right. I wasn't born yesterday. I get way up high and sit tight like I'm on the lookout for a deer. Comfy and quiet.

Officer Gallson walks to the left, then spins right like he's seeing ghosts out of his peripherals. He walks all the way over to me and wings his flashlight this way and that, but never *up* to my spot in the trees. He's standing a ways below my feet. I put my hand over my mouth to try and quiet my breathing, and get a taste of my salt-sweaty palm.

Just then, I hear a clatter. We both turn to look out at

the road. Officer Gallson's flashlight bounces around, but I can see a rock skitter across the shadows and into the ditch.

"Out in the open," Officer Gallson whispers. "Rookie mistake." He walks quietly through the trees out onto the road, I guess thinking that the rock is a person. I sit on that branch until my legs fall asleep. Until Gallson is way down Main Street, back at the car. It's then I realize I've been holding on to the branch in front of me so tightly that my hands feel wired shut. I clench and unclench them for a minute, stretching the joints, then I climb down. Once I reach the ground, I walk toward the *Mary Grace II*. I've only made it a few steps when I hear, "Hey, Indie?"

I turn, looking into the shadows. The goggles home in on Owen, *whir-whur.*

"Owen, did you do that?" I whisper back.

"Yeah, I followed you guys. I thought he was going to catch you."

"You threw the rock into the road?"

He winks as he steps out of a shadow.

"Thanks a lot for saving me back there," he says. "It wasn't very smart of me to go back."

I wave him off and head through the trees. Maybe Monty's still on the line. Maybe he saw it was us and stuck around.

When we get into the belly of the *Mary Grace II,* I grab the line and Owen does, too, and we haul it all the way up until it's swinging in front of us in the tree. But there is no Monty, just a couple of crabs skittering around the rope webbing. The soda bottle lies on its side. Most of the fish heads are gone; at least the bait bag looks pretty empty. I reach out and pull the trap in, then retrieve the crabs and chuck them out to sea.

"He's never coming back," I say, feeling defeated.

Owen takes the trap out of my hand.

"You know, my aunt Peg always says that getting something accomplished is twenty percent doing and eighty percent believing. Let's reset this trap."

He climbs down the ladder and I lower the trap down to him. Owen collects it in his hands and carries it back out into the waves. He tosses it as hard as he can, and his glasses almost fall off as the line zips by his face. As I look up to the sky, I think, Owen Stone might be a huge nerd who has a self-improvement plan, but as far as I can tell, he's the nicest kid I've ever met.

Chapter 28

AS BEBE AND I HEAD in to rehearsal, we spot Officer Gallson in the window of Crawdad Coffee House, sipping from a mug and eating a pastry. He's staring straight out toward the beach and the trees.

"He's relentless," Bebe says as we round the bend and head to the theater.

"Yeah," I say. Only she doesn't know the half of it. As we get close to Oceanside, Bebe and I run into Kelsey and a few of the von Trapp kids.

"Play it cool," Bebe whispers. "I heard the play next year is *Annie,* and I have a pretty good chance if I can keep this going." She lifts her right hand and starts chewing her nails. I swat it out of her mouth.

She drops it as the kids on the porch spot us.

"Morning, Bebe! Morning, Indie!"

"Morning, Chickorys!" Kelsey says.

One boy even sings good morning to us and I laugh as we walk up to the veranda. When I'm about to detach from

Bebe's side, she steers me over and we both sit down on the bench with the others.

"So, Indie," Kelsey says, sitting in one of the white rocking chairs. She crosses her legs and puts her hands on her knee. "You work downstairs, right?"

I nod.

"Do you see that Owen kid a lot?"

I look at Bebe and then out at the yard, wondering why Kelsey is asking me this. Wondering if he came up somewhere.

"I see him sometimes," I say, and I feel Bebe squirm on the bench next to me.

Kelsey pretends she's speaking into a microphone. "And would you say he is a loss, a complete loss or an utterly complete loss?"

The kids around me laugh as Kelsey pretends to hold the "microphone" under my chin.

"Huh?" I say.

"Is it a trick question?" Kelsey says, pulling the invisible mike back toward her.

"C'mon, Indie," Bebe whispers, digging her elbow into my side.

Kelsey holds the mike out again and everyone on the porch looks at me, waiting to see what I have to say, and my tongue is stuck in my throat.

Kelsey taps her leg as a few flowers spin down from the hanging plants. I watch them fall.

"No comment? Okay," she says, "next question. Do you think his parents rightfully abandoned him in Plumtown, or is there more to that story?"

"What?" I say, wondering where the heck she is getting her information.

Kelsey drops the mike then and leans in, being real Kelsey, not reporter Kelsey, for a minute. Ian and Bebe and the singing boy lean in as well.

"That's what I heard happened," Kelsey says. "That he's such a freak, they decided to pawn him off on his aunt."

"Wouldn't you?" Ian says, crossing his legs and leaning on the porch railing.

And Bebe does an extra-big snort and laugh. "Yeah!"

Kelsey says, "If he was my kid? I would have done the same thing."

Just as if on cue, Aunt Peg pulls into the driveway. Owen's sleeping up against the window, his nose smashing against it.

"Ew!" Bebe shrieks as they go over a bump and Owen's nose smears across the glass.

They all buckle over laughing and Owen pops awake. Bebe squeezes my arm and I let out a sort of laugh and scream at the same time, more out of surprise than anything else.

"So," Kelsey says, turning back to me. "Complete loss? Is that what you would choose for question number two?"

My stomach flips like a ship at sea and I stand up. Bebe looks at me and puts her hand up to her star charm. I look at her, wondering what the heck she is doing holding on to that.

"Yeah," I say. "I should go get ready to work."

"It's affirmative, folks!" Kelsey says, raising her hand. "A complete loss, he is."

I walk down the steps as they slap five and circle together for a warm-up. I make my way around to the stage door. As I get to the shop, it's like Sloth's waiting for me. She slams the door open.

"Chickory! Big day! You ready?" she says.

I jump back about fifty feet and hit the wall, causing one of the picture frames above me to start swinging violently.

"Oh yeah," I say, trying to sound amped up. I step in past her, surprised how quickly my stomach goes from rocky to calm in the presence of my scariest, most tattooed and body-pierced friend. It's funny, I think as I put down my bag. In the scene shop I kind of feel different, like there's more space around me. I can't quite place it, but I feel comfortable as we settle into our work, surrounded by saws and dust and music.

Chapter 29

WHEN I GET HOME, Mom must be thinking it's a pretty special night, because she's got garlic ginger mussels in the frying pan and a big baguette coming out of the oven. I take a deep breath as Bebe and I walk in the door and drop our bags.

"My favorite," Bebe says, going up to the baguette and picking a piece off the corner. Mom slaps her hand away.

I grab at it, too, but Mom snatches it out from under my hand and shoves it onto a platter. Then she goes over and pulls the top off the pan of mussels. She tosses a pat of butter and a handful of scallions in and covers it for a second longer, then she dumps the mussels, broth and all, into a big bowl. She puts it in the middle of the table. At the same time, Pa comes in the back door and puts his boots over to the side, taking a deep breath, too. I make a fish face over the bowl of mussels as I dive in.

Bebe scowls at me, but I ignore her. It's just one little face, after all. I peel off the empty half and suck the broth and pieces of garlic and the cooked mussel out of the other side. The garlic and ginger hits the back of my throat and warms my insides. Bebe eats hers daintily, prying the mussel out with a fork.

"You're losing the flavor, little lady," Pa says, but Bebe just shrugs. We eat the whole bowl of mussels, then Mom tears a chunk of bread off for each of us and we dip it into the broth at the bottom of the bowl. I take a bite out of the chunk in my hand. This is my favorite meal that Mom makes. Not even Mrs. Barkley can make a meal this good.

After dinner, Bebe practices her arpeggios and I watch the sun set, wondering if The Lobster Monty Cola is sitting in the trap underneath the *Mary Grace II*.

Bebe runs a few chords up and down the piano and I get up to go to bed.

"You want to watch the stars?" she asks, looking up from her keys.

For a minute I think I would like that, like old times, but since the costume shop incident and now the incident this morning, it's feeling half like old times and half like new times that I can't even enjoy.

"Nah," I say, "I'm tired."

"Really?" she says, looking disappointed.

"Yeah."

I kiss Mom and Pa good night, go into the bathroom and brush my teeth. Then I head into my room and shut the door. I go over to my window and sneak it open, quiet as can be.

I'm barely awake as I make my way outside. I sneak

around the house and grab a new bait bag, reach into the gunk and tuck some heads inside. I duck along the house toward the front yard but stop short in the shadows. There's a noise, like a window creaking open. I pause and lean against the house.

"Pisces, please," Bebe sings. "Pisces, please. Promise me . . ."

I peer up. She's leaning out her window, holding on to her charm and singing.

"Perfection. Pisces, please. Oh, please. Perfection."

She squints her eyes closed, the way you do with the most serious wishes. And in the shadows, I feel my stomach spin. I get that same-blood, same-bones feeling. And it's a heart-heavy sort of yearning. I watch as Bebe opens her eyes and puts her elbows in the window, resting her head on her hands. Downstairs there's a crash and Bebe spins away, looking into her room. I jump, too, nearly making a dent in the siding.

"Everything okay?" Pa hollers.

"Just dropped a pan!" Mom says back.

I look up to make sure the coast is clear. No one's standing in the windows as far as I can see. I book it.

Chapter 30

I DUCK ALONG the tree line, holding the brand-new bait bag, watching for old Officer Gallson and his rickety squad car. I look left and right, up and down Main Street. When nothing is there, I head across Crawdad Beach, then into the trees, making my way through the darkness. I know the way so well now, I jump over the downed log without even stubbing my toe and reach my hands out for the pine bough just as I get to it.

"Owen?" I whisper as I step out onto the outcropping of rock.

The flaps of his aviator cap swing over the edge of the platform as he smiles and waves. His cap has a sort of blue aura around it, pressed against the night sky.

"Indie!" he says. "There you are."

I climb the ladder and get up next to him.

"Check it out." He goes into the bow and pulls a rope through a pulley. I look closer. It's the trap line. The buoy slides down onto the floor of the tree fort as he pulls the line. The trap lifts out of the water on the other end.

"I rigged this pulley system so when we get a catch, we can hoist it much faster than last night."

I grab ahold of the buoy line, too. It slides smoothly up and down. Either of us would be able to pull it in on our own.

"That's awesome!" I say. I pull the trap up until it is hanging right in front of me, then tie the rope off quickly on a lower branch. I reach my hand into the trap and swap out the bait bags. The empty Coke bottle is still sitting inside, looking silvery, full of water and sparkles. Monty didn't have any luck pulling it free. But we still have the second bottle, which Owen opens. He pours half of it over the trap.

"There," he says. "All set!" Then we lower it into the water.

"Also . . ." He goes over to his backpack and pulls what looks like a mess of rope out of it. But once it's out in the open, I can see it's two big fishing nets.

"Where did you find those?" I say, going over and picking one up.

"From props. They were used onstage for *Pirates of Penzance*. I was thinking we could use them as railings. They'll provide more security."

He holds them out lengthwise. Then he pulls a staple gun out of the bag and starts stapling the net down the tree, along the platform and up the tree on the other end. I watch for Monty as Owen finishes one side and then the other. I swear I see a couple of tail flips here and there, but when I pull the trap up, there's no sign of him.

Finally, Owen sits down next to me.

"There's supposed to be a meteor shower tonight." He turns and looks at me. "Being a believer in such things, how many stars do you think I would have to wish on to fix something?"

"Something?" I ask. I wonder if maybe Owen really was abandoned in Plumtown. But that can't be right, because why would his parents come and visit him for lunch like they did the other day? I look up into the sky, wondering if I should ask or just keep my mouth shut. Finally, I decide I'd better not pry. "I guess that depends on the size of the problem."

"It's big," Owen says.

"I thought you didn't believe in wishing on shooting stars, anyway. I thought you only believed in executable plans."

"Yeah," Owen says. "True. But when that doesn't work, wishing seems like the next best thing."

One star streaks out across the sky. And as I turn my head, I see Owen watch it until it fades into nothing.

"Well, what's your wish?" I ask. "The faster you are with it, the better chance it has of catching hold."

Owen lies down on his back, folding his hands together behind his head. He shrugs.

"I wish I was good enough," he says.

"O—" I start.

"I wish I was good enough. To make my dad want to stay."

I watch a star start to fly, but it sputters out halfway like it's extinguished by the coolness of the night. This sounds big. I lie down, too, putting my hands behind my head.

"Stay?" I say.

"Yeah. My dad. If I was good enough, he'd stay. He's leaving. That's why I'm visiting my aunt Peg this summer. We're trying to, they're trying to"—he pauses—"figure it all out."

"Oh," I say, then I'm quiet for a minute, feeling his sadness roll in like the ocean. "Just wish on as many as you can," I tell him, reaching up to hold my Pisces charm, 'cause if there's a wish that could use some extra help, this is it.

"I suppose that will put the odds in my favor."

Owen closes his eyes and I watch the stars reflect off his glasses. Then I look straight up and spot Pisces in the sky. The fishnets coming up the sides make it seem like we're in a hammock. The trees sway as the sea breeze billows over us. The stars blink and blur in the sky. The *Mary Grace II* creaks, and even though we're not out at sea, I swear it rocks the slightest little bit from side to side. Over and over, I send Owen's wish off into the night, and then, without even meaning to, I fall fast asleep.

Chapter 31

TWEE-TWEE, TWEE-TWEE. At first I think I'm dreaming, something about being on a ship and nearing land, but as soon as I peel my eyes open I see shafts of sunlight cutting through the treetops. They're channeled into swirling beams of pink and orange as the fog and sunlight meet. I'm still in the *Mary Grace II* . . . and it's day.

I shoot straight up.

"Owen," I say, shaking his arm. "Owen." He sits up, fixing his glasses on his face. But while he's doing that, I grab ahold of his wrist and check his watch.

"It's five thirty," I say. Owen's bugging his eyes so wide, he looks like a scared ocean perch.

"Go!" Owen says. And we do. We shoot down the ladder so fast, onto the milk crate and onto the forest floor.

"Hurry!" Owen says as he bounds over to the pine bough. I jump in behind him and we both start jogging through the trees and the damp morning air. We hurtle over the downed log and over big roots, too. As we get closer to the beach, I tap Owen on the shoulder and put my finger to my lips. I point toward the beach and then toward my eye.

"Check for Gallson!" I whisper.

Owen nods and we slow down near the tree line, walking flat-footed across the leaves. Just as the sand and leaves meld together, we hunker down and take a look at the beach. The fog rolls off the sand like it's the earth's eyelids, slowly waking. Chickory and Chips appears like magic and Main Street, too, empty and quiet as can be except for a few seagulls flying in and out of the mist.

"We're clear," Owen says, and we duck along the tree line all the way up the beach.

Straight ahead is my road.

"I'll see you later," I say.

"Oh! Wait!"

I stop and turn back to him.

"I might be late. I don't know. Family meeting. Not sure if I'll see you at the theater, but I'll come back to the *Mary Grace II* tonight."

I nod, my heart bouncing like my feet should be, up the road to home.

"Okay," I say. "Good luck! See you tonight!" And we split and go our separate ways, Owen running down past Sandy's and me booking it up Brookrun.

I jog, checking over my shoulder every second. When I reach the house, Pa's truck is already gone for the day— he probably left an hour or so ago—but otherwise, the house looks quiet, not a light on. I run around the back and to the opposite side until I'm up against Monty's saltwater pool. I pop my head over the sill. My covers are still drawn over a pillow. I push the window open and climb in quietly. I peel off my shoes and socks and drop my Carhartts, then pull on my nightshirt. I run to the bathroom on tiptoe the whole way. And as I'm walking out the bathroom door, I stop. There's something. A tiny breath of noise coming from the vent over my head. Coming from Bebe's room. Upstairs. Just like the other night. I walk over so I'm directly under it and listen.

Is she talking, singing in her sleep? I look over to my right as there's the teensiest thump, like the sound of a footfall. I go to the bottom of the stairwell, grab the railing and step up the stairs as quietly as I can, trying to keep the weight in my chest instead of on my heels. I walk until I'm all the way to her door. It's open the slightest little bit. I put my eye up to the crack and look in, expecting to see her lying on her bed. But she's not.

Bebe's sitting on the floor, her pink room more purple with the bold morning light. A few wisps of fog run past her windows. Her white nightgown glows, rosy and spotless. She has her script out in front of her. If I didn't know she was rehearsing, I'd be really creeped out by the way she's staring into the dark of her room, talking ever so slightly. Practicing her gestures. She stands up, acting out an entire scene, falling into ballroom spins around and around the room. I cover my mouth, my breathing seeming so loud in the quiet of the house. Between escaping Gallson and leaving for the *Mary Grace II* each night, I sure am getting good at sneaking.

"One, two, three, one, two, three," Bebe says, barely above a whisper, but on three she stumbles the slightest bit and her hands fall down into fists at her sides.

"C'mon, Bebe," she huffs, then throws her hands up again to her invisible partner. "One, two, three. One, two, three."

I step back into the shadows of the hallway. I go down into my room and slide the door shut. Then I lay my head on my pillow and try to fall asleep. Only thing is, I can't. I just watch the fog peel away from the earth and the sky lighten up outside my window. After a while, I hear Mom shuffling around in the kitchen and then I hear a knock on my door.

"Yeah," I say.

Bebe comes in, smiling as big as ever, but this time, again, I see a little puffiness right under her eyes. Same as I saw at the coffee house. It just makes more sense now.

"Here you go," she says, handing me a black shirt with a bright white star in the middle. Smile, you're a star is written inside it. Underneath the shirt is a pair of light khaki shorts.

I roll out of bed.

"Thanks," I say, taking the clothes from her. I pull the

shirt over my head and pull my shorts on. I make sure my hair is parted neatly down the middle. As I go into the bathroom to brush my teeth, Bebe comes up next to me. My same-blood, same-bones sister. I know Bebe can be overdramatic, but maybe being the perfect actress is to Bebe what finding The Lobster Monty Cola is to me. Maybe it's the same heart-heavy-with-yearning feeling we have, just for different things.

Chapter 32

AS BEBE AND I HEAD DOWN Main Street, passing kids in strollers, fat old men with cameras hanging around their necks and ladies with fanny packs, I can't help but notice that Bebe is singing to herself a lot. More than usual. She seems nervous from the inside out.

"Are you okay?" I ask, stepping up onto the Chickory and Chips step, walking along it and stepping down on the other side.

"Fine," she says. "Only, listen, Indie, you really messed up yesterday."

"Huh?" I say, pushing my hands into the pockets of the shorts.

"Yesterday, Kelsey was drilling me on if you were friends with Owen, 'cause you were so weird in the morning."

I look down at the sidewalk and watch one block of concrete go by, then another and another and another.

"Just be cool, okay?" she says, grabbing on to my arm as we go. "*Annie*'s my all-time favorite musical. And it really looks like they're going to be doing it. If I stay close, I could be one of the lead orphans, or even Annie!"

"Got it. No problem," I say, hoping she'll stop chewing her nail.

When we get toward Oceanside, Bebe breaks off to the porch and I head straight across the grass and around the side of the building.

I walk in, past Mr. Bluesey's desk, and down the hall toward the scene shop. I pass the department doors. Mrs. Clark isn't in yet, but Aunt Peg is. I wave and she smiles. The rest of the office is empty. No Owen. I hope his family meeting is going all right. I walk into the shop and put my satchel down in the corner. Sloth is standing on the gazebo with a level running alongside one of the railings. She looks up at me, picks up the level and comes over.

"Are you having some sort of crisis?" she says, frowning.

"Huh?" I say.

She spreads her fingers wide and makes a circling motion in front of me, gesturing toward my shirt.

"I don't know, but judging by your usual wardrobe, SMILE, YOU'RE A STAR doesn't exactly line up."

Before she even finishes her sentence, I am pulling the earrings out of my ears and cursing myself for forgetting to change. I head straight for the satchel.

"Chickory, whoa!" Sloth says, walking along next to me. "What's the matter?"

"Nothing," I say, swinging the bag up over my shoulder.

Sloth grabs ahold of it midswing. She takes it and drops it on the floor. "Will you please relax? I'm not going to yell at you."

"You're not?" I ask.

"No," she says. "You're wearing sneakers, aren't you?"

I nod, looking down at the pink Pumas I snagged from the costume shop.

"It's just an observation. I'm not judging you. What am I? The fashion police? Do I look like I really care about your clothes?"

I smile as I glance at the fishing lures in her ears.

She turns, goes over to her bag and pulls out her iPod.

"But"—I hear a *clickclickclick* come through the speakers as she spins the playlists—"do you feel like listening to Weezer, Green Day, Bad Religion or Dropkick Murphys?" she says.

I walk over to her, picking the level up and putting it back on the railing of the gazebo. "Weezer, I think."

She smiles. "Predictable." A minute later the music is busting out of the speakers.

"We need to paint all our flats for the Alps scene," she tells me over the music, gesturing toward the flats that we laid out the other day. She heads toward four paint buckets over near the shop entrance and I follow. There, she hands me a screwdriver and I go and wedge the end underneath the lid. Sloth drops a few paint stirrers between us as she grabs another screwdriver and starts to undo the lid of another can.

"So, now that we're almost done with the prep, how do you feel about being backstage?"

"Huh?" I shout.

"Like, helping me backstage, during the shows?" she yells back.

I pry a lid off the blue paint can and scrape the excess paint back into the bucket. Then I lay it on the tarp below me.

"Yeah," I say, "maybe."

"Think about it," Sloth says. "You've been a big help this summer, I've gotta say."

She picks up a stirrer and mixes the gray.

"I'd like to," I say. "I just have to check with Mom and Pa first." Thinking that really I should check with Bebe so she doesn't flip like when I told her I was going to be down here.

Sloth nods. "No worries."

Sloth drops a dollop of the gray into a pan and adds a little green to it, then she shows me how to edge in the lines on the muslin. She shows me what paints mix well together into the shades of the trees and the mountains. And we listen to the music and paint and dance around a little bit while we're at it. Before long, it's time for lunch.

"Catch you in a bit!" Sloth says. She hits the loading dock door button and the door slides up, opening half the wall. She disappears into the brightness of the sun. I step out into it, feeling the warmth on my face.

"Hey, Indie!" I look out toward the front lawn and Bebe and Kelsey are both hanging over the side of the porch. Bebe waves me over.

"C'mere!" They both giggle, draping over the railings like roots over a cliff.

"Just a second!" I say. I go to my satchel and pull out the Tupperware. Then I step into the hallway, just to see if Owen made it in for the day or not. Aunt Peg holds up a small hammer and spins a chair around, hitting little nails into the fabric. When she spots me over the seat, she shakes her head at me.

"Not here, kiddo," she says, going back to work.

I guess Kelsey and Bebe are my best option. I go back through the shop and through the loading dock door, then head toward the front of the building.

"That can wait," Kelsey says, pointing toward my lunch. "I have something even more delicious."

Her eyes go big, and her smile is broad, but there's something a little menacing about it, like the face of a wolf-fish. Bebe smiles at me over her shoulder, her face brighter than a sunbeam. Kelsey takes one of my hands and Bebe the other and they lead me across the veranda, under the hanging flowers and into the dark of the lobby.

Chapter 33

"UNDER HERE," KELSEY WHISPERS as we come to the back of the bleachers. Big black drapes hang down to hide the skeleton of the bleacher unit, and Kelsey draws one drape aside.

"C'mon," she whispers as we step into the dark. I see Ian and the singing boy tucked up to the front of the unit, curled over in the shadows.

"What are we doing?" I whisper as we duck around braces, hunching down more and more as we get up to the front. "Are we supposed to be down here?"

"Oh, please. I own this place. I can go wherever I want," Kelsey whispers.

"Check it out," Ian says.

"Huh?" I ask, totally confused.

"C'mere."

We crouch down way low and peer out of a slit in the bleachers.

I hear Steve's voice come over the speakers. "House lights, please. We're back in ten." Steve's the stage manager. We don't see him too much downstairs but Sloth says I might as well get used to him because he's in charge of basically everything, especially once the show begins. And just as he finishes saying it, the house lights *do* come up. I can see Kelsey and Bebe better, even though we're still tucked into the shadows. Bebe has something in her hand. Not a string—it looks more like fishing wire. The wire we use to hang the picture frames, on set pieces, so that the lines can't be seen.

"What's that for?" I ask.

"Watch." Kelsey grabs my arm and pulls me to my knees next to them.

Actors and designers filter back in slowly. Some actors are stretching and others are warming up their voices.

I see Bebe look at Kelsey and Kelsey keeps shaking her head. "Not yet, not yet," Kelsey says, then finally she nods. Bebe pulls the fishing wire and I follow the line with my eyes, barely able to detect it as it lifts off the floor between the bottom of the bleachers and the front of the stage. It creates a straight line between the two, across the pathway where people are coming and going. And just as Bebe tightens it to the max, one of the girls playing a nun trips and barely catches herself on one of the chairs. Bebe and Kelsey both stifle a giggle and the two boys bend over gasping. Bebe releases the fishing wire so it hangs down again, lying on the floor of the theater. The actress turns and looks at the floor in a confused way, but she must not see it. So she keeps going.

"You do it, Indie," Kelsey says in my ear.

I shake my head. But Bebe starts shoving it into my hand. "Yeah, c'mon, you do it. You'll love it. They make the funniest faces."

Bebe raises her eyebrows at me. I give her a glare, hoping she's getting that this is the worst idea ever.

"Annie," she mouths. That makes my stomach twist, 'cause I don't want to do it, but then my stupid brain starts reminding me of this morning and all her hard work, and that this is a pretty simple way to be the best sister in Plumtown. This could make up for bringing The Lobster Monty Cola to school.

I nod. It'll be fine. My fingers wrap around the fishing wire and Kelsey does a silent clapping sort of hand gesture out of excitement. "I'll tell you when."

Bebe's face relaxes and I see her take a soothing breath.

I look over at Kelsey.

"Here, let me get this," she says, pulling out her iPhone. She points it at me. "Smile."

I smile. Not a real genuine one, but a little bit of one. Kelsey shakes her head several times as I hear people pass back and forth.

"Not yet, not yet," she says.

"Oh!" Her eyes fill with delight. "Now," she whispers.

I pull the wire.

"Yikes!" A familiar voice comes crashing through the bleacher wall. I look out and Owen's holding Styrofoam canisters, familiar canisters that look a lot like the ones that hold Chickory and Chips' famous clam chowder. He falls. The canisters fly. And then they come tumbling down, spilling chowder all over the carpet between the stage and the bleachers.

"You have got to be kidding me!" a voice hollers from right behind him.

I drop the fishing wire and jerk back, seeing Owen's dad through the crack.

"Jesus Christ, Owen. Do I look like I have time for this?"

He reaches down and grabs Owen by the arm and lifts him up out of the mess of chowder. He crinkles his nose and pulls a white handkerchief from his pocket to wipe his hands.

Owen looks up, stunned.

"Someone please inform maintenance that we need a cleanup right away," Steve says over the mike.

"Damn it!" Owen's dad curses.

"Sorry, Dad," Owen says quietly.

But his dad just turns around and walks out. And Owen looks down at the mess, a tear sliding down his face.

"Wow," Kelsey whispers. "That was epic. Look at the geek freak."

A chunk of driftwood lands in my throat. And it occurs to me that it could be me on the other end of this joke. But it's not. And somehow, either way feels just as bad.

Owen slips as he turns to head toward the stairs leading backstage.

Ian and Kelsey clap me on the shoulders like we're at a ball game and I got a home run, but their hands are just stinging and pushing me down. Owen slides in the chowder, trying to regain his footing, and finally runs.

The maintenance man comes around the corner and rolls his eyes.

"Let's scram," Kelsey whispers. And I'm in a tangle of arms as we reach the drape and sneak back out into the auditorium.

"That was fun," Kelsey says. "Hey, do you guys want to have a slumber party tonight?"

I'm not even hearing anything, just watching a bumblebee buzz around in the front yard.

"We'd love to," Bebe shrieks, jumping up and down. "You can come over. My mom makes the best fish stew."

Kelsey hugs her and then goes around the side of the bleachers.

"We did it," Bebe says. She hugs me. "*Annie,* here I come. You're the best sister ever."

But my arms don't reach up to hug her.

"I don't feel so good," I say. She steps back.

"You're not getting a bug, are you?"

I roll my eyes and go through the front door. The heat of the day smothers me. As soon as I'm out of sight of Bebe, I run around to the shop door. Part of me is rushing to see if Owen's okay and part of me wants to take a hike straight on home. Feeling ashamed from the inside out. By the time I get there, Owen's sitting in the gazebo, in the middle of the shop, and Sloth is pulling the first-aid kit off the wall. Some blood is running down Owen's knee. I slow to a stop and stand right next to the entrance, watching, afraid to go in.

"What happened, kid?" Sloth says.

Owen tries to clear his glasses from the fog and the tears.

"Brought some chowder for Indie for . . . for lunch—"

My insides twist like fishnets in the wind.

"But I tripped and dropped the chowder e-e-every-where." He blows his nose and Sloth pulls out a piece of gauze. "And my dad—" His voice crumples then. Crumples into tears and sobs.

"Shh, shh. It doesn't matter." Sloth shakes her head and dabs at Owen's knee with a piece of gauze. "It doesn't matter what anyone thinks."

Sloth's words blow over me like the wind coming in off the coast. My feet take me backward, reeling back, back, back out of there. Out toward Chickory and Chips and home.

Chapter 34

WHEN MOM'S WONDERING what I'm doing home so early, I tell her I'm sick and go into my room. And I am sick. At least I feel sick for being such a sour friend. I lie there in my room, looking up at the ceiling covered in glow-in-the-dark stars, and I can't stop picturing Owen spilling over. Again and again. I consider things. I consider my wish. Be a better Indie Lee Chickory. I consider myself. I get up and go over to my bureau, stare in my mirror hanging above it. Even though I might not be the fish freak of Plumtown anymore, I hate myself a lot worse than when I was. Sloth's words ring in my ears. *It doesn't matter what anyone thinks.* I pull the earrings out and throw them across my desk. Then I pull the shirt over my head, get rid of the shorts and put on some sweatpants. I grab a button-up, short-sleeved plaid and pull it on one arm at a time. The braids might look nice, but the breeze can't sift through my hair when it's pinned back like this. I pull the bands off the bottom. When I look in the mirror, I don't look real pretty, not like some made-for-the-stage beauty, but to me, it's an improvement. I try to make a happy clownfish pucker, but nothing happens except for the wounded mackerel. I slump into my chair and cry. I don't know how long I cry, seems like half of the day. I can't stop. Every time I try to, I see Owen falling, or his mean old dad yelling. I know that I have to do something to make it right. A confession. Only, when I look in the mirror and practice telling Owen, nothing works right. I'm too much of a coward to even do that.

I pull out a piece of paper. Maybe I can leave him a letter.

Dear Owen, I write.

I don't know if you can ever forgive me.

I scratch it out.

I'm the worst friend that ever lived.

Still not quite right.

You're the best person I have ever met.

That's right, but every time I get to the part about tripping him, I get jammed up.

"Indie!" Mom calls. "Bebe and Kelsey are home."

"'Kay!" I stand close to my door, hoping they don't try to come in here.

"You feeling any better?" Mom asks.

"Not really," I tell her, which is true.

"You want some soup, kiddo?" Pa hollers to me.

"No, thanks," I answer, leaning my head against the door. "I'll probably just throw it up."

I listen as Bebe and Kelsey make their way upstairs

and the giggling begins. I come out of my room and Mom hands me a bowl even though I said no, thanks.

I look at it and the smell wafts toward me. "Maybe just a little," I say, taking it.

"What's wrong, Indie?" Mom asks, feeling my forehead.

"Just queasy," I answer, ducking away from her.

I take the bowl back into my room and stare out my window. I sip the broth one teaspoonful at a time. Scooping up pieces of basil and garlic. And I hear them get dinner all laid out, then clink and clank their spoons in the other room. I watch the sky change from blue to Plumtown purple, then to dark blue, until the stars start to pop.

Mom knocks on my door and I dive into my bed. She walks in and over to me.

"How're you doing, kiddo?" she asks as I turn toward her, pretending to be half asleep.

She runs her hand over my forehead and this time I don't pull away. Her hand is cool against my skin.

"I'm okay," I tell her. "Just tired."

She gives me a kiss on the head and collects the bowl of soup off my desk.

"Get some rest," she says.

But as she closes the door, I slide out of my bed, turn my pillows so they're lengthwise, cover them with my blankets and go to the window. I climb out into the night and around to the front of the yard.

When I reach the road, I look back. Bebe's window is

all lit up, a glowing little sparkle in the night. I can see her and Kelsey silhouetted against the glass. Kelsey is wearing one of Bebe's dress-up hats and is brushing her hair pin straight. I can see Mom and Pa in the bay window. And everything looks as it should be. Just without Indie Lee Chickory.

Chapter 35

I HEAD THROUGH THE moonlight and into the trees. I'm going to tell Owen all about today and let him know what a big mistake it was and that I'll never make another mistake like that again. I hit my foot on a root and catch myself. I feel around and find the downed log. I jump over that and push past the pine bough. For a minute I am worried Owen found out what I did and didn't come, but then his head pops over the railing. He waves like everything is all right in the world. And I know that's not true. Not in his world. Not in mine.

I step onto the milk crate and climb up into the *Mary Grace II,* my stomach churning like spume in the waves.

Owen has pulled up the trap.

"Check it out," he says.

I walk over and examine it in the moonlight. The soda bottle is gone and the bait bag is only half full. I drop my hands. In all the worry I forgot to grab a fish head from the muck bucket.

"That's the last bait I have," I say, looking at it through the netting.

"Well, the trap came up with two crabs," Owen says, picking them up and putting them back in the trap. "Do lobsters eat crabs?"

"Yeah, he might go for them," I say. Then Owen picks up the half-full Coca-Cola bottle, dumps the contents in and ties the bottle inside the trap where the other one had been.

"I'll, uh, I'll push it out," I say, climbing back down the ladder and catching it as Owen lowers it. I drag it into the waves and chuck it as far as I can.

"C'mon, Monty," I say, then walk back to the tree boat and climb.

When I reach the platform, Owen has his Book of Logic and Reason out.

Self-Improvement Plan: Don't be a klutz, he writes.

"Hey, Owen?" I say. "You're not a klutz." I lick my lips and my knees start to shake the teensiest bit, so I sit down.

"Oh, but I am," he says. Then he puts his pencil behind his ear and looks up into the starry sky. "It's nice of you to say, but while you were home sick today, I had a major . . ." Owen pauses, looking down at his hands. "Just a stupid moment."

I stop for a minute, looking at his kneecap, looking at the gauze that Sloth put on it. Maybe if I don't tell him what happened, maybe if I just move forward in the right direction . . . But that doesn't sit right in my gut.

"Hey," I say, "I gotta tell you something."

Just then, the buoy swings on end and flips around. Owen jumps up and yanks the rope. I stand up, too, watching the rope run through the pulley. I get ready to grab the trap as it swings in front of us, but then the rope slams to a halt. I look over the edge of the bow.

"It's caught on that rock," I say.

"You got this?" Owen says, handing me the rope. "I'll set it free."

He climbs down and I lean back, letting my weight hold it in place. I watch as Owen scrambles over the rocks to the trap.

"Indie!" he shouts as he hauls the lobster pot out of the water and places it on the rock. I let go of the rope and look down at the trap. "It's Monty!" he says.

My heart hits my chest as he digs his hands into the lobster pot. I won't believe it until I see it. But as he stands back up and raises his arms out of the belly of the netting, I rub my eyes. Owen lifts him up into the moonlight. Monty. The Lobster Monty Cola.

"The aurum *Homarus Americanus*. In real life!"

"We did it!" I shout, forgetting everything else. I rush over to the ladder. But just as I'm putting my foot on the top rung, the whole world seems to light up. I fall back as a beam lights the *Mary Grace II* from below, casting shadows all around me.

I clamber to the railing, thinking it's Officer Gallson, but when I peer over, well, it's not. It's Bebe and Kelsey. They must have seen me leave. My hands drop to my sides as I watch my worlds collide.

Chapter 36

THEY PAN THE LIGHT from one end of the boat to the other.

"Indie, whoa! What is this?" Bebe says. "Can we come up?"

I look from Bebe to Kelsey and then over to Owen, who's standing on the rocks, still undetected.

"Who's that?" Owen says. I see Kelsey spin the flashlight so the beam is level to the ground. Her jaw drops and Bebe's brow folds in on itself as Owen lights up.

I panic. "What are you two doing here?"

"What's *he* doing here?" Bebe says. "What *is* this place?"

"And what is *that*?" Kelsey shrieks as Monty wriggles in Owen's arms.

"It's a golden lobster," Owen says, coming around to this side. "Otherwise known as The Lobster Monty Cola. He belongs to Indie."

"I thought you said you weren't friends with this nerd," Kelsey says, looking up at me. Pointing the flashlight at me and then down to Owen. We take turns shielding our eyes.

"What?" Owen says.

"I never said that!" I say nice and loud. Thanks to the light, I can't see Owen, but I sure hope he's hearing me.

"Yes, you did," Bebe says. "You said you didn't know him. You said he was a complete loss."

My knees wobble. "No, I didn't!"

"Is she nuts?" Kelsey says. I blink and see Kelsey and Bebe exchange a look.

"Can you guys go away?" I say, thinking that Kelsey and Bebe are going to ruin everything.

"Wait, I'm confused," Bebe says, putting her hand on her hip. "If you're friends with him, why did you trip him today? Why would you play along with our joke?"

At that, I hear a shuffle and Owen looks up at me. His face big and blue under his aviator cap. Searching my face. I can't do anything but look away as Monty squirms in his hands.

"Owen," I say. "Listen. I didn—"

"Yes, you did," Kelsey says. "I have video of it right here."

My stomach crumples, my insides turning into liquid. Stupid Bebe and stupid Kelsey and her stupid iPhone and her stupid jokes. I watch as she pulls it out. The stupid sparkly case glitters as the flashlight beam drops over it for a minute. Stop, I want to say, but it's like I swallowed a starfish and it's growing and pressing its arms into the sides of my throat, blocking out my whole windpipe.

"Owen," I manage.

But Owen walks like a zombie to the other side of her. He puts Monty down over his forearm and Monty seems to relax into the cradle of his elbow. The iPhone comes to life.

"See?" Kelsey says to Owen, pointing the screen toward him. She giggles as I hear the tripping scene happen all over again. Tinny voices come out of the phone. As I hear Owen's dad yelling at him, Owen's face scrunches up with pain.

"Listen, Owen. I was about to tell you. See, it was all an accident," I say, hanging onto the fishnet railing.

But Owen doesn't look at me.

"Owen," I say, turning and stepping onto the top rung of the ladder.

"Why?" he whispers.

Just then, the whole forest lights up. My foot slips off the rung, but I catch myself and straighten back up onto the platform.

A voice comes over a loudspeaker. "Everyone freeze." And I do. I stop right there, not believing any of this is happening. I turn my head and watch as the leaves rustle and the pine bough moves to the side.

"Let's go, kids," says Officer Gallson as he comes into the clearing. "The game's up. Your little pranks are over."

Bebe and Kelsey huddle together and Owen cradles Monty close to his chest. Officer Gallson looks at me up in the tree.

"You too, Chickory, let's go," he says.

I lower one foot, but just as I'm heading down, I notice that Owen has left his book. Owen doesn't go anywhere without his book, so I scoop it up and bring it along as I climb down the ladder. By the time I reach the ground, Officer Gallson has got everyone in a line. Owen's in front, then Bebe and Kelsey. I take up the rear. We head out of the woods.

The red and blue lights flood around us as we cram into Officer Gallson's rickety squad car. He puts Bebe and Kelsey and me in the backseat and Owen in the front. Tears slip down my face as I slide along the seat to the far window and Bebe jams an elbow into my side as she gets in.

"No rough business," Officer Gallson says, closing the door.

"Where are you taking us?!" Kelsey squeals in her most dramatic voice.

Officer Gallson comes around the side and gets in the driver's seat.

"I'm taking you home, where kids your age ought to be at this time of night."

So all of us have to tell Officer Gallson where we live, except for me and Bebe, 'cause he already knows that.

"I hate to do this to you," he says, "but there's been some real tricky business around here and I'm not tolerating it anymore. Crime is crime, and people who steal things and trick people"—he looks at all of us in the rearview mirror, his eyes darting back and forth—"are criminals."

I look away from him, out the window. Saving The Lobster Monty Cola is no crime, but I keep my lips sealed. Officer Gallson puts some music on as he pulls out toward Brookrun Drive.

"The Chickorys first," he says. And Bebe and I duck our heads. I cringe, thinking of what Mom is going to say, but more than that, I don't want to leave without Owen knowing that it was all a big misunderstanding.

"Owen?" I say, wondering if he'll listen.

But he doesn't say a word. I lean forward and peer into the front seat. Monty's looking up at Owen and sort of petting his arm with his claw. Good old Monty. He was always the best at helping out on a tough day.

"If you just listen to how it all happened," I say.

But he doesn't turn or say a word. It's like he doesn't even hear me. It's like he doesn't want to, and I don't really blame him.

I inch as far over toward the door as I can as we turn onto Brookrun. The blue and red lights spread out across the lawn, light up Pa's truck and the wood siding of the house as we pull up. Gallson lets the siren ring out. He's just doing it for extra effect now, I think. I see a light pop on in Mom and Pa's bedroom window. They both come rushing through the living room as Officer Gallson opens the door of the squad car.

"Let's go," he says.

My feet don't want to move, but Officer Gallson grabs my arm and steers me out of the car and up to the door as Mom and Pa spill out onto the porch. Bebe follows.

"What happened?" Mom says.

"What's going on?" Pa says.

Mom wraps us into a hug.

"Relax, Mr. and Mrs. Chickory. Everything's all right now," Officer Gallson says, but looking down at Owen slumped over in the front seat of that squad car, I think nothing could be further from the truth.

Chapter 37

I SIT AND WAIT in my room, feeling sick to my stomach and angry as a tidal wave. Stupid Bebe and Kelsey. And poor Owen. At least he's got Monty. I flip the corner of Owen's book, worrying for a minute as to whether Owen will know what to do for Monty, but if anyone can take care of him responsibly, it's Owen. I take a deep breath. It's going to be okay, I tell myself. It's all going to be okay.

A quiet knock comes and I let go of the book and go over to my door. My feet feel heavy, like my bones are made of chain.

"Indie," Mom says.

I open the door and spot Bebe going toward the stairs. I can't stop myself. I feel like I have fireworks in my brain. As soon as I see her without Kelsey or Owen around, I just let go of everything.

"What is wrong with you?" I shout. "I hate you! You're the worst sister in the whole world!"

She lurches back like my words are flinging her off her feet.

"Settle down," Pa says, putting his hand on my shoulder.

"She wants to be so perfect," I spit. "Well, she's not. Not even close!"

I take a deep breath and Bebe stares at me.

"All she cares about is her stupid self and her stupid play and being perfect. She's the one who messes everything up—not me!"

Bebe's face is pinching together like all the force is in the middle.

"Shut up, you—you freak!" Her hands ball into fists. I lurch at her, but Pa catches me.

"Enough!" Mom and Pa yell at the same time. Bebe thunders up to her room and I collapse into Pa's arms. Mom reaches down and pats my head.

"Can you take a seat, Indie?" she says. "We could use a little help understanding everything."

I hear Bebe's door slam and I hear her sniffling through the grate in the ceiling. Pa steers me over to a chair and I sit down. We wait for a few minutes and I take lots of breaths. One after another. Trying to breathe like the ocean.

"So . . . what happened?" Mom asks, looking at me from across the table.

I look down at my hands, not liking the way her eyes are trying to catch mine.

"Tell us the whole story," Pa says.

When I finally find my voice, I can't help but do just that. I tell them all about wanting to find The Lobster Monty Cola and stealing Mr. Crisco's golf cart and going to get the boat ends and working on the show and trying to be a better Chickory, and how it was nice to see Bebe really being my best pal like when we were little, but then how it all wound out of control and everything collided into a big mess I couldn't untangle, leaving me without a friend and without a sister and without The Lobster Monty Cola. I sink lower and lower into my chair until I am basically talking into my arm instead of to Mom and Pa.

Mom pushes a mug of lemon ginger tea across the table at me and I take a quick sip, but it doesn't calm me down at all. Instead, it just stings the inside of my mouth. Pa leans over and pats my arm and says it was nice to think of saving The Lobster Monty Cola and he wishes he had gone out looking for him with me more. And that he's real proud of me for bringing up the grandest catch of all time. But that's about all the niceness they can muster, I guess. 'Cause then they launch in with more. How disappointed they are in me for sneaking out, and in Bebe, also. I hear a little shuffle near the grate in the ceiling and I bet Bebe is being her nosy self and listening in on the entire thing.

"You'll have to keep off of Mrs. Parson's property," Pa says.

I can't help the tears sliding down my face.

"You're going to have to save up some money and help Mr. Crisco with repairs on his golf cart," Mom says.

"I'll be bolting your screen onto your window. Never thought I would have to do that." Pa shrugs. "But it's not safe for you to be sneaking off." He puts his face in his hands like he can't believe any of this.

"What about the play?" I ask, hoping I can get back to Owen tomorrow. To bring him his book and apologize and see The Lobster Monty Cola. Not that I deserve it. But that's what I want to do.

Mom and Pa look at each other. "We'll see," Mom says. "I'm not sure being in the scene shop has been the best influence on you. As far as I can tell, that's where half this trouble began. I've seen that girl down there. I'm not so sure she can be trusted."

"This has nothing to do with Sloth," I say, slamming my hand down on the table. Some tea from Mom's mug sloshes over the side and she gives me a warning glance.

"I'll have to speak with them, but until then, you should stay home."

Great. I've got nothing left. I wipe a few tears from my forearm where they've landed and are tracing their way down onto the table.

"Do you have anything else to say to us, Indie?" Mom asks.

"Sorry," I say, real quiet. 'Cause that's what you're

supposed to say. Everyone knows that. Really I'm not sorry. I'm just mad.

"Okay." Mom picks up her yellow lemon ginger mug. She takes a sip and a long breath in and a long breath out. "Go off to bed, then."

I push my chair back and lean against the table, still feeling heavy as ever. I head into my room and go over to my desk. I plop down in the chair and trace the words on the front of Owen's book. *Owen's Book of Logic and Reason: Observation Log IV.* I flip a few pages, spotting his self-improvement plan. I shake my head and rest my cheek on the cover, then turn my neck and peer out the window at the stars.

A shooter crosses the sky and there's only one wish I have in this whole world. And it's not for me. It's not for Bebe. I just wish that Owen could see how great he is, somehow. I send that wish up over and over and over again until I am fast asleep.

Chapter 38

WHEN I WAKE UP, I notice I have prints and creases on my face. I can't believe I fell asleep on my desk. I uncurl my shoulders and push against my cheeks with my fingers, trying to rub out the marks. I hear Mom and Pa talking to Bebe in the dining room.

"As soon as rehearsal is over, I will be there to pick you up," Mom says.

"Okay," Bebe says, her voice quieter than ever. My throat tightens up just hearing her. How can everything go so right, then so wrong so fast?

I go out and Mom wipes a dish as I sit down at the table. I look at Bebe, her face puffier than ever. Probably 'cause she's been crying all night. Who cares. She pulls her script out in front of her and does a few quiet scales up and down.

Mom puts a plate of pancakes down in front of me and I hear a scuffling from my room. When I look, I see Pa outside, setting the screen on the window. Then I see him pull the screw gun up and *whir, whir, whir,* he secures it on.

A car pulls up out front and Mom looks over to Bebe. "Time to go, Be," she says.

"Have fun at rehearsal," I say, not meaning it at all.

"I won't. Thanks to you." She goes over to the mirror and checks to make sure her hair is perfectly in place.

I dig a fork into my pancakes. "You know," I say, pouring some maple syrup over the top. Her hand stops primping her hair. "You and Kelsey just pick on other people's problems because you can't deal with your own."

Her hand flicks then, a piece of hair falling down by her ear.

"Indie, please," Mom says.

But I can't stop talking. "It's not that Owen's any worse than you or me. It's just that Kelsey's the type of person that has to pick on people like Owen and me to make herself feel better. I think that's pretty crummy. She's the last person I'd want to be like."

Bebe looks away from me then, her eyes filling with tears. She tries to comb her hair back into place as the car outside starts honking the horn. Mom puts her hands around her temples and forehead, like she's trying to push a headache out. I spot my face in the water glass. The crinkles are pressed into my puffy cheeks and my face looks wide in the bend of the glass.

"Everyone has 'em," I say. "Problems, I mean."

"Leave me alone." Bebe flips an elastic around the end of her braid.

"My pleasure," I say as she runs past me out onto the porch.

The door slams.

"Indie, go to your room," Mom says.

I take a bite out of my pancake.

"I said go to your room!" she says.

I take one last bite and go into my room. Pa double-checks the screen and then comes around the house. I lean on my desk and think about Owen and Monty. I've got nothing to do but think on all *my* problems. I trace fish designs over the cover of Owen's book with the tip of my finger.

"Bat ray, round ray, English sole, gray sole, rex sole, starry flounder."

I flip the corners of a page, just to give my hands something to do. It's only by accident that I see my name. I flip them again, and when I see *Chickory,* I stop and slide my finger down the page. Then I lay the book open in front of me.

> <u>*Indie Lee Chickory*</u>
> *Stats:*
> *friendly*
> *funny*
> *nice*
> *makes good fish faces*
> *knows the name of all the fish*

searching for the golden lobster
smart
believes in magic
friend

Tears start sliding down my face. I wish all these were true. A breeze blows in my window and my tears flick off my cheeks like the hands of the wind are trying to wipe them away, and at the same time it flips the pages of Owen's book over until it lands on a blank one.

I look down at it and it occurs to me that maybe I can show Owen how good he is—not with a letter, but with something else. I pull a pencil out of the jar on the edge of my desk, press the page flat and start scribbling.

While I write, I hear the phone ring a few times.

"I'm sorry, she can't talk right now."

"No, she won't be in today."

"No, sorry. She's out."

All three calls are for me and I get to wondering who it is, but it doesn't stop my progress. Eventually, I put down my pencil and push the book neatly closed. That's when I hear a little noise. I look out my window, wondering if maybe Owen came back with Monty and how great that would be.

A spiky head pops up over the bottom sill. I blink and pinch myself, but the image through the screen is clear. It's Sloth. She's got an X-ACTO knife in one hand and she's holding a finger up to her lips. Some might think that's scary, but now that I know Sloth, it's the best thing I've ever seen.

"What are you doing?" I ask in a voice that's quieter than a whisper. "How did you find me?"

She just shakes her head and starts cutting the screen. I can't believe this is happening.

"I can't," I whisper. "I'm going to be dead meat." She draws the X-ACTO knife all the way over so that a perfect semicircle drops out, then she leans her head in and I put my head up close to hers.

"Listen, Chickory. Bebe told me to come and get you."

"Bebe did?" I whisper. "I'm not going anywhere. She wants them to send me away to juvie or something."

"No," Sloth says, shaking her head. "She seemed really upset." Sloth reaches down and pulls Bebe's Pisces charm out of her pocket. She holds it up, and it spins at the bottom of its leather cord. "She said to give you this." I reach out and take it in my hand, running my thumb over the stars. "She said to let you know she heard something about Owen leaving."

My head snaps up, and my heart tries to hit the top of my head. I'm out the window before I realize it, grabbing the book and ducking around the back of the house, silent as I know how to be.

Chapter 39

"WHAT'S GOING ON?" Sloth whispers as we cut along a few hedges and out onto Brookrun.

"Did she say when?" I ask.

"No, she just said you might want to know and you'd better hurry and that I'd better break you out. She even drew me a map. Do you want to expl—"

"No time!" I hold up a hand, and even though Sloth might be skeleton thin from all her animal-free foods, there's no way she's going to run faster than me. We're busting through the doors at Oceanside Players before I know it. I thank Sloth at the door and head straight to props.

"Aunt Peg?!" I say.

She looks up at me, startled. "Oh, boy. What are you doing?"

"Is Owen here?"

She leans over a piece of Styrofoam, hot glue gun in one hand and black fabric in another. "I'm afraid not, darling. He's packing and then heading to his new home in

Sentinel. Seems . . ." She pauses. "Seems like they've made a decision."

"Packing—okay!" I start running down the hall. Then I stop and run back, realizing I don't know where I'm going. "Wait. Where's your house? I have to talk to him. It's really important."

"Now, Indie, I don't want one single bit of trouble today," she says, pointing the glue gun at me.

"I promise, Aunt Peg. Cross my heart."

She looks up toward the ceiling and shakes her head like she has a friend in the fire alarm who she's conversing with. Whoever's up there takes forever to agree. I jump up and down like Sloth does when we listen to her music, trying to shake some energy out. Finally, Aunt Peg sighs a long, drawn-out sigh.

"Five Blue Jay Crossing," she says. And I am out the door before she even finishes, because it's three streets over and I'm moving like a freight train.

When I reach Five Blue Jay, it looks exactly like it should. Exactly like something eccentric Aunt Peg would live in. There're a few solar panels on the roof and an antique birdbath in the yard. I run straight up to the front door and ring the bell. I watch my back in case Mom and Pa noticed I'm missing already and sent Officer Gallson out after me. I tap my foot for twenty seconds to give Owen time to get to the door, but he doesn't show up, so I start knocking. I wait twenty more. Still nothing. I check the garage and run around the back, but there is no answer. Then I look in each window, and it sure looks like no one's home.

I missed him. I can't believe it. I can't stinking believe it.

Unless . . .

I figure I have one more place to look before I give up hope.

"Push it, push it, push it," I say. And I run faster than I ever have before. Out toward Crawdad Beach. To the *Mary Grace II*.

"Owen!" I shout as I stumble and scramble in through the trees. "Owen?"

No response. I push the pine bough out of the way and climb up the ladder to the platform. Just as my head reaches over the edge, I see Owen. Monty's sitting on his lap and he clip-claps his pincher together when he sees me.

"Owen," I say. "Thank God I caught you."

"Hey, Indie," he says. He looks up at the ocean, and the straps of his aviator cap swing in the breeze. "I wanted to drop Monty off here and pick up my other things. I'm leaving tomorrow."

"Yeah," I say, sitting down next to him. "Bebe, uh, sent me a message. Listen, I'm so sorry," I start, but Owen shrugs.

"Please, you didn't do anything wrong, and I don't

blame you. It's pretty common knowledge that I'm a big embarrassment, a disappointment."

"That's where you're wrong," I say, taking Owen's hand and putting his book into it. He wraps his fingers around the binding, looking puzzled, probably as to why I have it, but I just barrel on, hoping he won't be mad. "The tripping prank was a stupid joke that Kelsey thought up and I swear I didn't know it was you coming around the corner. I thought you were out all day. You're not a klutz at all."

Owen smiles. "Thanks, but I *am* a klutz," he says, handing Monty over to me. I give the good old lobster a quick check to make sure that he is okay. His claw is regenerating well, and he leans up as soon as he gets into my arm and smooshes his pincher claw against my cheek. I smile down at him.

"My dad's leaving," Owen says. "I guess my wish didn't come true."

I set Monty in my lap.

"You're not the reason your dad's leaving," I say to Owen, taking the book back out of his hand and flipping it open. I sift through to find the page I've been working on. "Your dad's leaving because he has problems of his own."

I take the book and lay it flat between us, pressing it open so that Owen can see it.

Owen looks down at the page. "What's this?"

"You're so busy making self-improvement plans and writing down everyone else's stats that you never took the time to write down your own. And since you never did, I did it for you," I say, looking away, hoping he's not going to be mad that I wrote in his book. "Uh, so you could see the straight facts."

I watch while he considers the page.

> *Owen*
> *Stats:*
> *kind*
> *genius*
> *gentle*
> *caring*
> *determined*
> *nice*
> *great at ideas, innovations and executable plans*
> *deserving*
> *perfect*
> *open to new theories*
> *good at wishing*
> *best friend*

"Those aren't facts," Owen says, looking out at the water.

"They are," I say, "at least as I see them. And anyone who doesn't see them that way doesn't know you and doesn't deserve to be part of your life."

He runs his hand down the page and holds it gently between his fingers. The breeze lifts the corner and hits it against his thumb. I hold my breath and wait, hoping beyond hope that he believes the list as much as I do.

"Thanks, Indie," he says.

Monty lifts his crusher claw and clip-claps it in the air, and I give him a little extra squeeze.

"Just because other people are jerks doesn't mean that there's anything wrong with the rest of us," I say, looking down at the golden lobster. "Take Monty, for instance. He's unique, and we love him."

Owen nods then, pushing his glasses up onto his nose. A tear slides down his cheek. "I don't want to go," he says, rolling his book in his hands. My throat binds up, like I have knotted ropes inside it.

"I wish you didn't have to," I manage.

"Mom says we're starting a new life. Out in Sentinel."

I feel tears drip down my face. They fall onto Monty's head and roll over his shell and onto my leg. He pets my arm with his claw.

"Do you think you'll ever be back?" I ask, looking up at the waves, trying to breathe with them.

Owen twists so his feet are off the platform but propped up in the bow. Once I say it, the question hangs out there, hangs out there with the sun and the clouds, suspended over the water.

"Aunt Peg says I can come back summers and help her with the props. I mean, if I want to."

"Do you want to?" I ask, holding out my hand, hoping I know the answer.

"Affirmative," he says, taking it in his.

"You're my best friend," I say. "Forever, Owen."

He squeezes my hand. "Forever, Indie."

And we sit there and hold hands for a while, just me and Owen, watching the sunset streak the sky, letting the breeze flow through the *Mary Grace II*. Just being Indie, and Owen, and Monty for a while.

Chapter 40

Four Weeks Later

The audience erupts into applause as Sloth and I peek through the curtain.

"Standing ovation, baby!" Sloth says, patting my shoulder. Monty, who's sitting across my arm, raises his claws and clip-claps them together. His regenerating one makes a lot less clatter than the other. I scan the audience as the last people rise from their seats. It's the final show and Owen promised he would come.

"There's the nerd," Sloth says, pointing down toward the front row. And sure enough, there's Owen, standing and clapping. Aviator cap and all. He turns like he sees us watching him, then spots us here in the shadows. He stops clapping to wave. The stage lights fade down and the house lights fade up, and everyone breaks into motion, grabbing their purses and programs.

I watch as the work lights come up onstage and the actors and actresses flood down the stairs to change. Bebe comes darting over to us. She looks at me and throws a trout pout my way, and I mimic it. Her face splits into a smile.

"I'll meet you downstairs in ten?" she asks, starting to pull the ribbon at the back of her dress as she goes.

"You betcha!" I say, and Sloth and Monty and I head down toward the scene shop. We walk in the door and Sloth makes a few notes on her clipboard. I set Monty in the saltwater bath that Sloth has made for him, but he scrambles to get out, so once he's soaked, I pick him back up and put him on my arm.

"Really nice job, Chickory," Sloth says, setting the clipboard on the workbench. She goes to the iPod. "Street Dogs?" she says.

"Yeah," I say, walking over to the loading dock door as she presses play. I hit the door button and it slides up, spilling light and lyrics out into the world.

"Not without a purpose, not without a fight. I've got three tales to tell you, so please sit tight. It's a story of three underdogs who've grown to see their light . . ."

Sloth walks over and leans against the door frame. Me and Monty lean on the other side, staring out into the dark. The smell of the sea mixed with the geraniums and foxgloves rides along on the summer breeze.

"Hey, hey, Indie! Sloth!" Owen hollers as he comes running around the side of the theater toward us. We hug and Sloth claps him on the back.

"Good to see you, little man," she says.

"Great job. Everything went off without a hitch!" he says, pressing his glasses up on his nose.

A second later, Bebe comes through the shop from the other side. Her face is still flushed from the show and her hair is still pinned up in curls, but she's wearing her shorts and a T-shirt. She's carrying a few bouquets of flowers.

"See?" I say, giving her a one-armed hug as she comes up to us. "You don't need any 'networking.' Looks like you do all right all by yourself."

She smiles, spilling the flowers out onto the ground. Sloth flips the shop light out so the only thing slipping out into the night is the steady beat of the Street Dogs. The sky is so full of stars, I worry that it might grow tired of holding all of them and spill them down to us.

"Hello, Pisces," me and Bebe say at the same time, spotting our constellation in the sky. Bebe raises her arms out wide and twirls in the grass, Owen pulls his book out to draw the constellation in his most current observation log, and Sloth nods her head, spikes bopping to the beat of the music. I look down at The Lobster Monty Cola as he rolls over to sleep on my arm, then I gaze back to the heavens and find Al Rischa among the other stars.

"Hello, Al Rischa," I whisper under my breath. I clasp my Pisces charm with my free hand, and just then, something occurs to me. I think maybe Pisces kept her promise all along, and I just didn't get it until now. Here with Sloth, Bebe, Owen and Monty, I *am* better. With the souls who understand me. I'm the best Indie Lee Chickory I can be.

ACKNOWLEDGMENTS

There are a multitude of people that helped in the creation of this book. First, I would like to thank my online critique group, made up of the unreliable narrators Barbara Crispin, Cynthia Vaughan Granberg, Jennifer Wolf Kam, Sarah Wones Tomp and Sharry Phelan Wright, who took a look at the first pages and started me on the journey. I would also like to thank my VT Crit group, Tamara Ellis Smith, Cindy Faughnan, Kerry Castano and Trinity Peacock Broyles, who let me talk and cry and who picked me up, turned me around and pointed me in the right direction. Thank you to my EMLA and VCFA communities, whose intelligent and inspirational voices echo through my day-to-day. Thanks also to Jessica Dainty Johns, Amber Moulton and Trent Reedy for random check-ins and writing days. Your motivation and encouragement is invaluable. As always, thank you to the EMLA team, especially my wonderful agent, Ammi-Joan Paquette, who urged me on in the beginning and championed the novel. Thanks also to the whole team at Philomel, especially Kiffin Steurer and Michael Green, and my unstoppable editor Jill Santopolo, who guided me from the beginning to the end, asked all the right questions and saved Owen from an early demise.

Of course, there are so many people to thank who encouraged me or inspired me directly or indirectly as I worked with Indie and Owen. Those people are my dear friends and family, especially my sisters Casey, Moie and Ambs, who have an amazing way of showing me what it is to live and strive. Of course, my parents, who are always a beacon of creativity, light and love. And to my Howie, thanks for always being there to support me in my writing endeavors, but also for being a great brainstormer as well as a logical opinion when my ideas begin to spiral. You are the greatest.

Turn the page for the first chapter
of Erin E. Moulton's
sweet sister story . . .

flutter

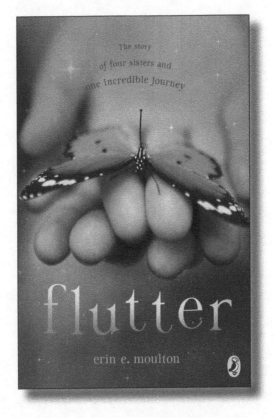

Chapter One

It all starts at home. On the mountain. Three miles up a rut-ted dirt road, out past Mr. Benny's apple orchard and over the hill from Nanny Ann's farm stand. It's fall now, my favorite season. And in just a few days, we are going to be having my favorite holiday: Halloween. Yep, out here on Canton Creek Turnpike, it's time for candy collecting and pumpkin carving.

Papa's prepping my pumpkin, and I am looking out the window. The sun has almost set, leaving the world soaked in streaks of orange and heavy purple shadows. It's the best time of day, with everything turning gold.

The swing set, the river, and the already fallen leaves melt together in the dusk. Our ox, Millament, is walking lazily toward the barn. Going to get warm, I suppose. I bet he wishes he was in here, and I sorta do too. The fire is crackling in the woodstove and the house is alive with noises: Mama humming in the kitchen, sisters fussing around the table, and Papa slicing away at the top of that pumpkin.

I'm about to come away from the window and get started, but then a little glimmer of brown flits in and out of the shadows and for a minute it looks like a leaf tumbling in the wind, out of control, but then it lands just below the window and I can see it's a genuine monarch butterfly. I put my hands up to the glass because that monarch is crazy to be out there this time of year. She wouldn't have the proper amount of meat on her bones to survive. I'm breathing quick and thinking maybe I had better go and get it to come inside, but I fog up the window with my breath and when the fog disappears, the monarch's gone. I hope it's headed south and not trying to prove it can make it through the winter.

"There you are, kiddo. Get started," Papa says.

I turn toward him. He wipes his hands off on a kitchen towel.

I go over to the table and pull the top off the pumpkin. I put it down next to me. I am about to dip my hand into the mushy insides when Beetle, my little sister, comes running around the corner of the counter. She holds a small gourd to her belly, then she teeters and totters to the edge of the table and throws it on the floor. It thuds but doesn't crack. She squeals with glee and picks it up again. This time, she heads straight for our mutt, Curious, who snoozes by the woodstove. Not for long, though. A second later, Beetle drops the gourd right next to Curious and he lifts his head and stares at her with a what-do-you-think-you-are-doing look. Curious and I are genuine friends, so we have good eye communication, and I can tell he wants this business to stop right now so he can relax.

"Come on, Beetle, don't bug Curio," I say. She picks the gourd up and carries it to me. She'll probably start drooling on my leg or something, 'cause that is what babies do. They don't have control of all their body yet. She hangs on to my leg, and I pat her on the head and look across the table.

Dawn, my older sister, sets down her knife. She's all done; her pumpkin has been gutted and carved. It stares at me meanly.

"Don't copy mine, Maple," she says.

Like I would want to copy hers anyway. I am going to make a real masterpiece. Dawn wipes her hands and opens her book. It's a journal, and Dawn writes all

her thoughts in it. I've read almost all of them. There is
a little spot behind the bottom drawer in her desk. She
puts it back there where she thinks no one can find it.
But I know it's there, and sometimes candies are there
too, which I like just as well. I haven't read any of it this
whole week, so I peer with eyelids almost shut at her
book. That way she doesn't know I'm looking.

*Trevor Collins is the worst kid in my class. Just because your
dad is the park ranger doesn't mean you know everything there is to
know about the woods. We went outside yesterday and he*—Dawn
slams her forearm across the entry just as I start getting
involved.

"Quit looking at my paper and carve your pumpkin,
Maple," she says.

I sit back in my chair and ignore her glare. I think
about carving the best pumpkin in town. Two days before Halloween, the Bee's Nest, our general store, empties
out its parking lot of all the cars and sets up big pumpkin
stands. Everyone in town brings a pumpkin. The whole
place seems to glow orange, and some of the pumpkins
are real amazing. Last year, there was one with the town
center on it. I figure I will try something like that. I dig
my hand into the pumpkin's belly and start loosening
the seeds. You have to really pull to get them all out, and
you have to dig around with the top of a mason jar to
clean it proper.

Papa sits at the end of the table and puts his glasses on his nose. He flips through a worn-out field guide called *Birds of the Northeast*. He looks up and says, "And the Latin name of the cardinal is—"

I plop some seeds into a bowl of water in the middle of the kitchen table and Dawn and I say, "*Cardinalis cardinalis*." Of course, that one's a cinch. They aren't all that easy, but I've memorized a bunch of them so far. Papa makes us learn a new one every Sunday. Other nights of the week we review the ones we already know.

I dig my hand in again and chuck some pumpkin seeds into the bowl. This time, a little bit splashes out accidentally and lands right on Dawn's page.

"Maple!" Dawn's face gets red, and she jumps up and starts dabbing at it with some newspaper.

"Jeez Louise, I didn't mean—" I start to say, but she picks up her journal and walks to the other end of the table, near Papa. He doesn't look up. He just keeps flipping the pages of his book. He's pretty involved.

"Mama, did you see what Maple did?" Dawn turns and holds her book up to the light.

"It'll dry, Dawn. You know it was an accident," Mama says, and I smile inwardly knowing Mama's on my side. I look over at her where she stands in the kitchen, her apron dusted in flour. She is making something that smells real good. I think it's going to be sticky and sweet and covered in frosting that I can lick off the tips of my fingers. She slaps some dough on the counter and looks at me.

"Do you want to come and help me work the dough?" she asks.

I toss some more pumpkin seeds into the bowl and wipe my hands off on my shirt. Mama grimaces. I come around the counter and she has already got a stool out for me to stand on. I step up onto it in front of her. Her arms come around me and I can feel her big belly and the new baby kicking inside. Mama says babies grow the best when they know that there are good things waiting on the outside for them, so we have to be supportive of it and talk to it a lot. I rub it and feel it under Mama's skin.

"Time to make the dough, baby," I say. Then I spin around to help Mama.

"Just like this," Mama says, and she pushes her palm into the dough. Then she lets me have a try. The flour is soft on my hands, but soon the dough gets stickier and we have to add more. Mama sprinkles the flour down and sings in my ear.

> *From the sky she fell*
> *Softly in the trees.*
> *If you gather round I'll tell*
> *Of Old Lady Hope, you'll see.*

Old Lady Hope will soothe,
Wise Woman of the Mountains.
When wind and rain and sleet do swell
Collect water from her fountain.
Pure waters from the mountain.

Mama's been teaching me this song one verse at a time and I am to the point where I know nearly the whole thing. I thump the dough with my palms and pitch in my voice too. I can feel the singing from the tips of my toes to the tips of my fingers.

Seek her out in times of plight
When you don't know where to start.
She is where the answer lies
Follow with your heart.

"Mayel," Beetle says. I didn't even know she had made it all the way over here until I feel the stem of the gourd jab right into my foot.

"Beetle, don't do that," I tell her and kick at her a little bit, but she looks up at me from her spot on the floor and starts giggling like something is hilarious.

I feel Mama laugh and the baby pats my back, but I keep on going, pressing my fingers into that nice soft dough.

Full of water, wind and sun,
Hold your head up high.
Deep within the mountain's song
You will hear her sigh.

Love and love and round we go,
Clasp your hands and sing.
Round and round and round we go
To form the healing ring—

"How's the rest go, Mama?" I say. Mama chimes in with her sugar sweet voice:

Water, sun, moon, and rain
Will do their part to heal.
Still greater powers come to call
When love brings strength, concealed . . .
Love and love, the purest love
He—

"Agh." Dawn slams her book shut. "It's so loud in here. I am going to go light my pumpkin."

I hit the dough some more as Dawn gets her fleece jacket out of the closet. She grabs gloves and picks up her jack-o'-lantern.

"Can I have the lighter, Mama?" she asks as she stands

at the door. And I hope Mama says she cannot have the lighter, but Mama looks over at Papa. He gets up out of his chair.

"I'll come out with you, Dawn. Hang on." Papa grabs Beetle away from my feet and puts a little jacket on her, and then they hurry out onto the porch.

"Mama, can I—" But before I even finish, Mama is wiping my hands off with a washcloth.

"You go ahead, little one," she says.

I run to the closet as fast as I can and get the first coat that touches my fingers. It's one of Papa's red flannel jackets. I shove my arms into the big holes and head out onto the porch with the others. The stars are out and clear as crystal.

Papa lights a candle and passes it to Dawn. "Now just lower it in—"

"I've done this before, Papa," Dawn says and lowers the candle into the grinning jack-o'-lantern. Once the candle settles, she puts the cap back on sideways. I can smell wax and burning pumpkin. An orange glow lights our faces and hands, and I step a little closer to get some warmth on my fingers.

Papa stands up tall like he is listening real close, so I put my head up too and search with my ears. I hear something far off. It's nothing but a whine at first, then it gets bigger and bigger. Coyotes! Lots of them.

One minute we listen, and then my papa fills his lungs full and lets out a howl straight into the night sky. It's so cold his breath puffs out in a long billowing line. I'm thinking it's crazy for a minute, then I set in too. I don't know why, but it's the best feeling when you're screaming into the sky and you're not sure if it's your own voice coming back at you or someone or something else answering your call. Beetle starts waving her hand in the air and tries to make the sound, but she's one and a half, and she hasn't got it quite right yet. She sounds more like that annoying dog at Mr. Machetee's, just down the road. Dawn is two years older than me. She's eleven and a half, and I think she might be getting too old for this howling, because she keeps rolling her eyes and sighing.

Anyway, there we are howling, and my voice, or something, is flying right back in my face when Curious starts making a big fuss indoors. I catch a glimpse of him in the bay window. He's got his nose up against the glass and it's smearing and smudging and his paw is up and scratching. I've seen him do this before, but something is different about it. His ears are all perked up, and his eyes are going wild this way and that.

Then I hear a big crash, and Papa is running inside so fast you wouldn't believe it. Beetle bounces up and down in his arms and, of course, starts to bawl. Papa hugs her to his chest and runs out of sight. We are out on the porch, Dawn and I. Dawn just looks at me and the coyotes yip and yap, and Curious barks and scrambles, and I hear Papa's steps pound up and down and all around the house.

All of a sudden, everything is still for a moment, and then I hear Mama. I hear my mama like her voice is coming through a long tunnel, and it starts out as a slow quiet moan and then it gets louder and louder. I run before I even find my legs, because I look straight into Dawn's eyes and I can be sure something is really wrong. I can be sure nothing has been so wrong in my entire life. Dawn darts in front of me. The bottoms of her shoes flash like the white velvet of a deer tail.

I run through that door, and there is Beetle on the floor crying next to my mama who is also on the floor crying. Her belly pops up like a huge balloon. Papa has got Mama's face in his hand and he looks down at her and talks quiet and breathes fast. Seeing everything so abrupt like this makes my knees start to shake, and I'm not sure what to do. I'm breathing fast from running, and my hands flap and my toes curl and my heart hits my chest like a woodpecker on a birch tree.

My papa talks to me, but I can't hear him above the pounding. His mouth moves and his eyebrows come down in the middle and, well, he says something, see, but I don't do anything 'cause I'm not sure what's going on. But Dawn listens and she can hear something and she runs into the other room and she's got the phone in her hand. I have Beetle in my lap now, and I try to calm her down 'cause tears are coming down her cheeks like raindrops in April. I pat back her curls and kiss her on the angel kiss on her head.

From my spot on the floor I can see my mama's face real close. It's scrunched up, like when she is mad, but there is something else there. I grab her fingers, which are white and dusty from flour.

"What's the matter, Mama?" I ask.

"Nothing, baby. It's nothing. Just pregnancy pains," she says. She gives my hand a squeeze and tears roll out of her eyes and mine too. I put my hand on Mama's belly to see how the baby is doing. *Thump thump*, little feet kick against my palm. *It's not time yet*, I think. I rub her belly and try to make it calm, but something shudders and patters against my fingertips, my thumb. The thumping grows lighter, softer, weaker. *What is it?* I think. I put my ear down to hear. The sound is hollow when I close my ear on Mama's stomach. *BompBompBompBomp*, HelpHelpHelpHelp. Help. *I'm listening*, I think, but hands grip me below my armpits. They pull me to my feet.

"Wait," I say, but strangers have ahold of me, and my voice gets stuck inside of me. They turn me around, and the room tilts and twirls. They push me out. But I stand at the edge of the living room and crouch down so I can peek around the corner of the sofa.

Papa takes Beetle and holds her to his chest. His face is wet with tears, and he talks to the people who walk into my house. They've come with a rolling bed and a loud truck. Everyone rushes around. The people in uniform stomp on the floor and push things out of the way. A chair knocks against the table and my half-gutted pumpkin teeters and rolls onto its side, spilling a gob of seeds across the kitchen table. Dawn is crying, and Beetle is screaming and Mama is huffing like she is having a hard time catching her breath. Before I realize it, my legs are taking me straight out of there. They take me up the stairs and into my rosy room. Only it isn't so rosy. The lights are bouncing off the walls, making everything blue and red, and the colors fill my eyes.

I peer out the window, and I see them roll Mama along the driveway and into the back of a truck. I don't know if it is my imagination or what, but all of a sudden my attention goes to the screen right in front of my face. A set of wings is beating and battering at my window. They flutter sporadically and I am frozen stock-still wondering what the heck it is. It being dark and the end of autumn, reason would tell me it's a bat. But I am looking at it, and it's much too small to be a bat, doesn't have enough flutter to be a moth. That means it's only one thing. A butterfly. All I know is something must be really wrong if nature isn't acting the way it ought to.

My throat tightens up and I am not sure, but it's awful hot in here for such a cool autumn night. Those butterfly wings change from blue to red, back and forth they flicker. My feet start jumping and I turn and run. I grab Paddington Bear right off my bed, head straight to the linen closet and scoot myself in among the soft sheets.

There are no lights here. The screaming of the siren is less, and I can hear my own breathing. The sheets, they smell like comfort. Fresh and clean. I wrap myself up in them. Then the tears come again, and all I can think of is the baby fluttering there in Mama's stomach, scared. My palm tingles and I picture baby footprints imprinted on my hand. I hear her cry in my head. *BompBompBompBomp,* HelpHelpHelpHelp.